Praise for

*"Absolutely breathtaking –
a dazzling and very scary novel"*
Kevin Crossley-Holland

"A heart-pounding, intense read – hold your breath"
Sarah Mussi, author of *Siege*

*"Should secure Ruth Eastham's place among
the very best of British children's writers"*
Caroline Green, author of *Dark Ride*

"Hits the ground running and never lets up"
**Paula Rawsthorne, author of
*The Truth About Celia Frost***

*"A thrilling supernatural adventure weaving
skilfully between past and present"*
Katherine Langrish, author of *Dark Angels*

"A fantastic read!"
Matt Dickinson, author of *Mortal Chaos*

Ruth Eastham was born in the north of England and has lived in several different UK cities, as well as New Zealand, Australia and Italy. Her award-winning novels, *The Memory Cage* and *The Messenger Bird*, are also published by Scholastic.

www.rutheastham.com
www.twitter.com/RuthEastham1

ARROWHEAD

RUTH EASTHAM

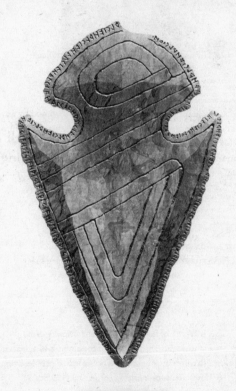

■SCHOLASTIC

First published in the UK in 2014 by Scholastic Children's Books
An imprint of Scholastic Ltd
Euston House, 24 Eversholt St
London, NW1 1DB, UK
Registered office: Westfield Road, Southam, Warwickshire, CV47 0RA
SCHOLASTIC and associated logos are trademarks and/or
registered trademarks of Scholastic Inc.

ISBN 978 1407 13793 3

A CIP catalogue record for this book is available
from the British Library.

Printed and bound by CPI Group (UK) Ltd, Croydon, CR0 4YY
Papers used by Scholastic Children's Books are made
from wood grown in sustainable forests.

1 3 5 7 9 10 8 6 4 2

www.scholastic.co.uk

For
Anna, Tom, Elena, Evie, Leo, Giulia, Jacob and Aileen
Cousins of the Clans

I remember the mist of our past.
As I speak to you in the present,
My ancient eyes
See the terrible future.

The Doom of Odin

PART 1 - ICE

PART 2 - THE PLAGUES

PART 3 - EARTH AND FIRE

The dying boy crouches in his ice prison.

His breathing is thick and short, and blood seeps through his grey cloak, turning to red crystals in the bitter air. The wound is deep and he knows he has little time.

The boy heaves himself to his feet with a cry of pain and looks up the sheer walls of the crevasse to the jagged hole he fell through. He tries again to climb, clawing at the impossibly slippery surface. Flakes of snow swirl downwards from the opening. The blizzard will block it soon. Already the light is fading.

He grips the golden arrowhead, using its tip to write on the wall of ice. The razor edge scrapes and grinds as he carves out the words. The freezing metal has welded to the skin of his hand, but he does not stop.

He must write a warning. A warning about the arrowhead he holds. Why it must stay trapped, deep underground, never released.

The boy sinks back, shaking. He thinks of his people in the village at the edge of the water, the ones who are already dead.

Sobbing a little, he lifts the arrowhead again. The cold seeps through him like poison. It is hard to think; hard to breathe, but he knows he must finish the runes. The threads of light are almost gone, but the dying boy continues his task, forcing the arrowhead again and again into the lifeless ice.

PART 1
ICE

↑

1
NORTH

The wise man is never parted from his weapons.
VIKING SAYING

"*Troll Boy's dead!*"
"*Fight! Fight!*"

Excited shouts shot round the playground as the mass of kids waited. School was about to end and, just for the fun of it, Lukas Brudvik was going to beat up the Troll.

"At least use his proper name," muttered Jack as he hovered by himself at the edge of the group, shifting from one foot to the other to keep warm. He zipped his padded jacket to the maximum.

What had got into those kids? They'd been all right up till now. Welcoming even. It was the first time he'd seen anyone bother Skuli. It was like someone had flicked the "mad" switch; cast a spell on them or something.

Where were teachers when you needed them?

Stay out of it, Jack told himself. If they were picking on Skuli, that meant they weren't picking on the screwed-up thirteen-year-old new kid from England. Him.

Jack stabbed the toe of his trainer into a puddle, breaking its brittle cover of ice. This was supposed to be the start of the summer holidays? This place made even British summers look good. But then what did you expect when your mum dragged you to Norway and a town virtually in the Arctic!

Jack brought up the last message on his phone, from Vinnie back home.

Need you back in goal! Just got slaughtered 3–0!! You owe me a bag of chips.

Jack smiled. Then that familiar feeling gripped his chest. He'd only been in Isdal a few weeks, but already Northumberland and footie matches with chips after seemed a long way off and a long time ago.

He quickly tapped a reply.

Can't wait 2b back. Am freezing 2 death!

Shouts rang out. Jack slipped his phone back in to his pocket. The words rippled round the mob. *Skuli's in the cloakrooms. . . He's putting on his coat. . . That Troll Boy's dead. . . Fight! Fight!*

Jack watched the kids, screeching and hooting, chanting for Skuli, while the show-off, Lukas Brudvik, strutted about, making a big show of putting on gloves and flexing his fists.

A girl in a blue coat turned her head and looked at Jack. She wasn't doing any chanting. A long plait dangled from under a fur-trimmed hat. What was she called? Emily or something. . . *Emma*, that was it. He knew what her look was saying. *We should do something.*

Now all eyes were on the cloakroom door. Jack could see Skuli through the window, standing by the coat hooks, still folding those little origami animals he'd been making in class, his mass of curly black hair flopping over his face, oblivious to what was waiting for him.

"I'll let you have a go at the Troll if you like, Jack Tomassen. Soon as I'm finished." Lukas Bruvik was by his shoulder. He nodded and his smirk said, *Prove yourself, new boy. Here's your chance to pass the test. You can be one of us.*

Everyone went quiet. The door swung open and Skuli came out, blinking at the knot of kids in his way. They parted and he stepped forward, still fiddling with one of his origami animals.

Lukas circled Skuli, his boots slapping the frosty concrete, his arms behind his back. "*Troll Boy. . . Troll Boy. . .*"

Skuli Isaksen was half troll – that's what Lukas had been telling everybody that morning. That was why he was short and stocky. That was why he and his dad kept to themselves and lived under the ground, in a basement flat under an abandoned shop.

Jack's heart thudded. He felt the kids' impatience, taut and dangerous, like the drawn-back string of a bow. He saw

5

Emma, trying to make herself heard over the din. Lukas marched in time as he kept on with the chant. "*Troll Boy. . . Troll Boy. . .*"

Others took up the words. Some moved slowly towards Skuli. The others clapped their hands as they sang, moving in a circle, closing in. Kids who Jack would never have expected to copy a loser like Lukas.

Emma was shouting now – "*Stop it! Leave him alone!*" – but their chanting drowned her out.

Lukas darted at Skuli, then jumped away swinging a bunch of nettles. The kids around him scattered, laughing. Skuli rubbed at his face and Jack saw red blistery lumps come up in a line by his mouth. Lukas swiped at him again and Skuli nearly fell as he tried to get out of the way.

Jack stood there, his hands clenched in fists inside his pockets. Skuli could get rid of Lukas with one good punch if he wanted. He was small but he was strong; Jack had seen him in sports lessons. One good, well-placed punch where it really hurt. . . But there he was, not even trying to defend himself. Why didn't Skuli fight back?

I should just walk away, Jack told himself. *If Skuli won't help himself, why should I?*

But now Lukas had a stick, a thick thing covered with thorns. The other kids were hollering. Emma was jostled away as she tried to step in. The stick swiped through the air and Skuli gasped. A line of blood appeared across his forehead.

Jack's body tensed. That was going too far. Skuli could have had that in his eyes! *Walk away now,* the voice inside him said. *Find a teacher. It's nothing to do with you. Keep out of it.*

Lukas lunged and smacked Skuli's face with his fist. Skuli shrank down, covering his head with his useless hands.

The crowd screeched. Lukas stood back, looking pleased. "Want a turn now, New Boy?" he called to Jack.

The crowd went still. All eyes on Jack. The wind sent a sheet of newspaper flapping across the concrete. Just one little slap; that was all it took, he told himself. Score some points in the new boy stakes. Be accepted into the Isdal clan. He wouldn't have to be the weirdo outsider any more. He nodded slowly and stepped forward. *I can be best mates with Lukas and live happily ever after.*

Jack launched himself towards Skuli with a shout, but at the last second he swerved and rammed into Lukas instead, pushing him hard, making him slam down on his backside. The other kids howled with laughter and Lukas lashed out at them as he tried to get up.

Jack grabbed Skuli's arm. "Go on." *Don't stare at me like I'm the thick one!* "Get out of here!"

Jack turned back to Lukas and helped him to his feet. "Up you get, Lukie." *This little New Boy is going to show you where* you *belong . . . in the emergency room of the nearest hospital!*

Lukas glared at him, shaking him away, and then Jack noticed the other kids, re-massing, moving in. There were more sticks. Big stones now too.

Skuli still stood there like a moron. He tugged at Jack's sleeve. "We'd *both* better get out of here, don't you think?"

A fist-sized pebble slammed Jack's leg, nearly knocking it from under him. Another thumped hard against his arm. *What had got into these kids?* The crowd moved closer. *So many. Too many.* Jack swallowed and moved back a step. Faces staring, hostile. *Two against thirty?* He didn't fancy those odds.

Jack sprang away, dragging Skuli with him. *I'd have a better chance pulling a dead body along with me,* he thought.

Instantly there was a rush of children behind. "Quick!" They hoisted themselves over the playground fence. Jack lost his footing and slammed down on to sharp gravel. He scrambled up and ran on across the playing field. The kids streamed after them. There were short shouts, little screams of delight; Lukas at the front, yelling.

Jack sprang over the drainage channel at the end of the field and pelted up a grassy slope. He reached the crest of the hill. A smooth long finger of water stretched out in front of him, pointing at the sea. He saw the fishing boats bobbing on the metal-grey water of the bay, the blood-red houses huddled on its banks. To the right, brown fields sloped downwards; to the left was the wide, wooded valley, another hill rising up behind it, with a tall wooden church on top and the river gorge beyond.

Jack sped straight down towards the town, calculating the distance they needed to cover: the grassy slope; the long, narrow tracks through the scrubby pine woods; on to the main street. . . Thank god for all that football training back home; that's all he could say.

Jack twisted to check on Skuli. He was falling behind.

The other kids were gaining, pouring over the lip of the hill. Behind them was the vast dark rock of the mountain that loomed over Isdal with its pitted glacier.

"Faster, Skuli!" Jack shouted.

He plunged into the labyrinth of tracks that twisted through the woods, passing a crow impaled on the barbed wire fence: a warning to other birds not to come near. Gusts of wind snatched at his back. What had he told himself? *Walk away. Nothing to do with you. Keep out if it.*

Jack whirred round. Where was Skuli? He couldn't see him anywhere. *Great!* Jack started back.

Skuli must have taken a different path. Had he got away? Jack could hear the thud of feet nearby. He ran faster, speared by spiky twigs. The path branched in different directions. He passed the burnt-out wreck of a smashed car, thick tufts of grass and twisted bushes growing from its rusty bonnet. The path branched again. Was it right or left? His mind buzzed with confusion. His breath came out in bursts. The pine trees seemed to be closing in around him. He chose a track and veered down it. Where was Skuli?

Jack glimpsed kids through gaps in the trees. Each thump of his trainers on the hard ground jarred through his body. He passed the burnt-out car again. *Stupid!* He'd gone round in a circle! And then someone was looming up right in front of him, one hand raised, in a fist. . .

Lukas.

Jack tumbled and rolled to one side to dodge him, his back scraping painfully against the rough bark of a tree. He saw Skuli standing nearby, watching with a frown. *Thanks for the help!* Jack scrambled to his feet again. He wiped the sweat from his eyes and saw the stone in Lukas's hand.

A heavy stone with a sharp point. Lukas shifted it from one hand to the other, then raised it above his head, as if getting ready to throw. Sticks with thorns and oversized pebbles was one thing, but this. . .

More children arrived, bunching up behind Lukas and then fanning out round Jack and Skuli. The branches above shuddered and the wind hissed menacingly through the pine needles.

You didn't throw big rocks at people's heads. Even dense bullies like Lukas must know that.

Jack stood firm. "Want to kill me, do you?" he said, forcing himself not to flinch. But he felt little shivers on the back of his neck. There was something in Lukas's eyes. Something unfeeling. Something frightening. Jack took a step back, trying to keep his voice steady. "A *murderer*, are you?"

Skuli shot Jack a look of alarm. Lukas raised the stone higher.

There was a flurry of movement. Right over their heads, a bird was thrashing about and shrieking, like its wings were tangled in the branches.

Lukas was distracted for a second and Jack saw the cruel look slip from his face. He dragged his eyes away from the branches and stared at Jack, and the stone in his hand, as if he was wondering how it got there. Then he let the rock fall like it had scorched him. It hit the ground with a dull thump.

"Lucky you've got your mummy looking after you, Troll Boy," Lukas said quickly. He kicked a shower of dirt at Jack. "I won't forget this, Foreign Face. 'Cos that's what you are, isn't it? A loser foreigner with a dead dad.

"Dead dad loser," he hollered as he strutted off, the other kids drifting with him. "Dead . . . dad. . ." The words seemed to swirl in the wind, coming from every direction at once.

Jack stood watching Lukas go.

Dead dad.

He clenched his teeth. Why did he have to say that? He'd rather Lukas had thrown that rock at his head.

"Thanks," Skuli said. "And sorry. I'm not very good in a fight."

Skuli stood there with his hands in his pockets, black hair flopping, staring. Really staring, as if he was trying to work something out. Jack scowled back. Didn't Skuli realize how close they'd been to having their heads smashed in by a rock?

Skuli gave a shaky laugh, then edged closer. "Your Norwegian's good."

"I am Norwegian. But I was born in England. My mum and dad are both from h—" Jack's face went hot. "My mum is from here."

"Oh."

Skuli carried on gawping, like Jack had two heads or something. It was creeping him out big time. "You're just like him," said Skuli, the words bubbling out. He glanced round as if checking who was listening. He inched even nearer and lowered his voice. "At first I thought it *was* you. That you'd been messing about up there and had fallen."

What was he going on about? "Fallen? Up where?"

Skuli opened his mouth to speak, then shut it again. "Oh, nothing. Nowhere."

"Whatever." This Skuli was obviously a nutter. "OK, I have to get home now."

Jack started to walk off, but Skuli had hold of his arm suddenly, gripping it, making him spin round. He was looking at Jack, his eyes wide. "*When the hands of children murderers be.*"

"What?" Jack shook Skuli off.

Skuli shuffled back. "Sorry." He looked away, flustered. "It's just a poem. An old ballad or something. My gran made me learn it years ago. I've forgotten most of it now, but lines just pop into my head sometimes." He tried a smile but there was a troubled look fixed on his face. "Sorry," he said again.

Jack twisted a pine needle in his hand to try and stop his fingers from trembling. When the hands of children murderers be. That rock. Lukas. The look in his eyes before he'd dropped the stone. If there hadn't been that flapping bird, distracting him. . . "Those kids are mental," he muttered. He rolled up a trouser leg and rubbed at the dried blood on his knee. "Let's get home."

Skuli gingerly touched his head where Lukas had smacked him. "He shouldn't have said that about your dad."

"Let's get home, I said."

They walked together in silence along the track, Jack tensed up for any sign of trouble. They passed the end of Church Lane and saw the first few houses at the end of the main street.

"Look, Jack." Skuli took a paper bird from his pocket – one of those ridiculous things he'd been making in class. He pulled the tail, and the wings flapped so delicately that Jack couldn't keep himself from grinning. "You try."

With a sigh, Jack took the bird. Up and down the wings went, in jerky little movements. Skuli burst out laughing, nodding his head, and Jack found himself laughing too. Something about Skuli reminded him of Vinnie.

"You should tell your dad what happened," said Jack. "Maybe he'll want to have a word with Lukas's dad or something."

Skuli's face fell. "My dad's away," he muttered. "But you won't tell anyone, will you?" he added quickly.

"Why? How long's he been away for?"

"Only since two days ago. He's got a mountain rescue conference in Oslo. It's really big; they only have it every two years. And then he's going to talk to some restaurants there – see if he can sell his catches to them. We really need the money."

A mountain-rescue fisherman? Jack frowned. "So who's looking after you then?"

"No one." Skuli tugged at a lock of hair. "I'm old enough to look after myself for a few days! Dad thinks so too. Anyway, he left me money, and loads of food in the fridge and. . ."

"OK, OK," said Jack. A kid at home alone. Big deal. It happened all the time. It wasn't as if Skuli was five. "Your dad shouldn't have left you though." He thought about his own dad and there was that familiar little stab in his chest so he had to turn away. "Your secret's safe with me."

"Thanks." Skuli gave a laugh of relief. "I knew I could trust you. I could tell. Soon as I saw you."

Skuli paused and his face went all serious. He was staring intently at Jack again, and then he looked worriedly along the empty street. He unzipped the front pocket of his coat and took something from it. Something wrapped in newspaper. Jack got glimpses of headlines. *FREAK WEATHER CONTINUES. COLDEST SUMMER ON RECORD.*

Skuli hesitated, then held the bundle out. Jack took a step back, almost stumbling. "What is it?"

"Take it!"

There was something in Skuli's voice; something urgent, pleading almost. Jack breathing speeded up without him having any idea why. He looked at the bundle in Skuli's hand. Somewhere overhead there was a flurry of wings.

"Take it," whispered Skuli.

Jack curled his fingers round the bundle. He lifted it into his palm.

The breeze tugged at the cuffs of his jacket, strong and raw, but the wrapping was warm, as if there was something alive underneath. Jack slowly peeled away the layers, the newspaper dropping to the ground.

Inside was a piece of golden metal. It fit his palm exactly, and was strangely warm against his skin. Heavy too. Maybe it was real gold? He lifted it to the light, his mouth dropping open. "Amazing," he heard himself say. The gold had a brilliant sheen. Delicate patterns curved across its surface, the twisting lines fusing so you couldn't see the start or the end.

A pattern of tiny lines was engraved around its edge. Jack couldn't take his eyes away. It looked like old Viking writing. Runes. He ran a finger over them.

"Careful," said Skuli. "It's dangerous."

He showed Jack the line of a half-healed wound on his hand. "I got cut the first time I held it. Really deep, though it healed super fast. I think it's from an arrow – though it's pretty weird to use gold for something like that."

Nodding, Jack peered at the engravings on the golden arrowhead, nicking his skin as he turned it over. Scarlet beads of blood trickled in a line along his hand, but he hardly noticed. He liked the way the warm gold felt, and his fingers curled over it protectively. . .

Then the church bell struck. A single dull clang that quivered through the air, pulling Jack out of his trance.

"Half past five," Skuli said to himself.

"Here," said Jack, "take it back." He tried to hand the glinting triangle to Skuli, cutting himself again in his haste, deeper this time. Dark red blood oozed across his wrist, smearing over his skin as he tried to wipe it away.

Skuli shook his head.

"*I* don't want it. . ." said Jack. His heart hammered with

panic, but a weird kind of thrill too. He found himself putting the arrowhead into the chest pocket of his jacket and zipping it up. "Where did you get it from anyway?"

Skuli leant close and spoke in a whisper.

"In the ice."

Jack blinked at him. "The ice? What do you mean?"

Skuli's voice was hard to hear. "Yes. The ice. And there were other things too." Then there was that troubled look on his face. The wind pulled his hair into thick black tufts. Overhead the cables between telegraph poles were jumping tautly from side to side, like whips. Skuli looked Jack straight in the eye.

"*The plague of air will be the start.*"

He looked away. "Sorry. Something from that stupid poem again. Can't get it out of my head." He was looking past Jack, down the street, then suddenly he spoke right by Jack's ear, his voice curious and afraid. "But you *do* look just like him."

"Who?" asked Jack.

Skuli eyed some kids hovering at the far end of the street. "Can't talk here. Come on. I'll show you."

"Wait," called Jack, but Skuli was already moving fast, turning up the steep lane that led to the church.

Jack stared after him. *Half five*. He should be tucking into cake and hot chocolate at Gran and Gramp's *kafé* by now. Sno, his dog, would be waiting for him, and there'd be nobody spouting creepy poetry.

He felt the arrowhead, heavy by his chest. *From the ice.* But where? What was the big mystery?

"I have to show you – now!" Skuli called back without stopping, bending his head into the wind.

"Wait!" shouted Jack. "Skuli!"

And the cloud shadows slipped along the pavements after them, slick as mercury, and the tiny shadow of a raven circled high up in the sky.

2

THROUGH THE GRAVEYARD GATE

There'll be wild weather, with windstorms dreadful.

THE GREAT LACUNA

"Skuli!

Wait, can't you?"

Why couldn't he have put on this kind of speed when the mob was after him?

The plague of air will be the start. No wonder he was Skuli-no-mates, going on like that!

Jack had to sprint to catch up. As he turned up Church Lane, he saw colourful bunting strung between telegraph poles and a ragged poster flapping on a lamppost:

ISDAL'S WORLD FAMOUS
FESTIVAL OF THE MIDNIGHT SOLSTICE
*STARTS IN JUST **TWO** DAYS!!!*
HOT FEAST, BONFIRE, FIREWORK SPECTACULAR
GO BACK IN TIME. . .

Where was Skuli taking him?

"Wait! *Skuli!*"

The lane wound up to a few parking spaces on the edge of a graveyard, which was spread over a saddle of land attached on the base of the Brennbjerg mountain. The dark wood walls of the stave church loomed over the cemetery, crosses and dragonheads jutting from its roofs.

Jack followed the path as it weaved between the gravestones. He thought about the arrowhead. Maybe it was stolen? Maybe Skuli was scared of being caught with it? If it was real gold it must be worth a lot. Jack veered past an angel with a missing wing, shuddering as he brushed against its cold stone. Where *were* they going?

Skuli paused at the far end of the graveyard, glanced back at Jack, then disappeared into a knot of spindly trees.

Jack pushed his way through the rough branches and spiky leaves after him.

"Skuli?" he called, struggling to see ahead as he stumbled on. His hands batted something spongy but solid. An overgrown wall, crawling with moss and ivy. He heard Skuli call to his right and followed the wall to a rusty gate with bars and spikes, half hidden by thorny stems. Skuli stood on the other side, holding the gate open. Once Jack had passed, the wind swung the gate closed with a drawn-out whine and a click.

Beyond the gate was a standing stone higher than Jack's head, completely covered with lichens. Skuli turned away and started to climb a narrow snaking trail. Jack followed him, stepping carefully through the gully of loose rocks.

After a while, the track opened out into a steep-sided, shadowy valley, fringed with immense, grooved granite boulders. Behind them the church bell clanged, and there was the sound of rushing water, getting louder as they picked their way upwards.

They were right at the foot of the mountain now. Jack caught his breath as he stared at the jagged rock cliffs above him. They walked on, finally coming out on a wider path he recognized. There was a splintering wooden board with a date, 1870, and the words EDGE OF GLACIER. Every so often there was another board with a date, marking the shrinking edge of the ice. 1880, 1890. . . The date boards got closer and closer together, so you could see how much the melting must have speeded up.

The sound of water turned into a rumbling growl. They rounded a bend and came to the bank of a river, racing dark past them and down the valley. The melt river of the Brennbjerg glacier.

The glacier. Ice. Hadn't Skuli said he'd found the arrowhead in the ice? Jack shuddered, but he didn't have time to stop. Skuli was walking fast and he'd lag too far behind if he did.

And anyway, how would he explain how he was feeling to Skuli? What would he say? *Sorry, Skuli, I don't do ice. Can't stand being anywhere near it. Can't even bear ice cubes in my Coke.* Which one of them would seem the total loony then?

But he felt the strange heaviness of the arrowhead pressing against him through his chest pocket.

Jack cursed under his breath and hurried on.

The melt river ran fast beside them. Floating chunks of ice swept past. Jack tried to squeeze out the rising panic and recall facts; a lesson with his geography teacher back home.

A glacier is a river of ice, flowing slowly down the mountain. . .

Ice can stay in a glacier for more than a thousand years. . .

Pressure compacts the ice and turns it blue. . .

And then they rounded another bend and Jack stumbled to a stop, caught his breath. There was the glacier, stretching up the mountain and out of sight.

It wasn't the first time Jack had seen the Isdal glacier, but it was more spectacular than he remembered. It was the angle of the sun maybe; the way the pale light was seeping over it, making the gashed sheet glow silver and sapphire.

Skuli turned to him, beaming, and Jack forced a smile in return. He felt the glacier towering over him as they approached; the immenseness of it. They were right up close to the frozen ridge now. Water thundered from the dirty hem of ice at its base. The streams flowed into the wide melt river that slicked away.

The rope barrier that separated the path from the cliff lurched in the wind like a manic skipping rope. A metal sign had been driven into the rock: DANGER. There was a picture of a stick figure falling amid jagged tumbling shapes.

Skuli dodged under the barrier and made his way towards the side of the main face, where the ice was buckled grey against the polished rock. He began to climb the high, jumbled pile of boulders, like they were giant steps.

Jack stayed at the bottom, cupping his hand to shout to Skuli. "What, we're going *on to the glacier*?"

"Yes. Come on!" Skuli beckoned him impatiently. He stood waiting on a thin ledge of rock, his face pinched with cold.

"You can't be serious!" He must be mad. You didn't walk on glaciers. Not without the proper equipment; not without a guide. The same way you didn't run across motorways. No way.

"We won't be on the actual glacier," called Skuli. "Not really. Anyway, I've been up here loads of times. It's safe. Well, kind of."

Stop being feeble, Jack told himself. *Rather sip cocoa with your granny, would you? Skuli says its OK. His dad does mountain rescue, so he should know, right? Don't you want to find out where he found the arrowhead?*

He stepped slowly past the wooden DANGER sign with its falling stick figure. He eased himself under the twitching rope barrier and started to climb the rock slope.

What's the worst that can happen anyway? He smiled to himself grimly. *You step on a crevasse hidden by a thin layer of ice and fall hundreds of metres to your gruesome death. Nothing much to worry about really.*

"Follow where I put my feet," Skuli called back. "Keep to the rock."

Then he was gone, dropping suddenly over the top of a slanting crest of ice.

"Skuli?" called Jack, his stomach turning over with fear. "Where are you?"

Skuli's face bobbed above the white slope, then disappeared again. Jack scrambled up the snowy incline after him.

He found himself on a wide platform of granite jutting from the valley wall into the edge of the glacier. The flat area had been shielded from view from below by a bulge in the wall of rock. Skuli was crouched at the far side of the platform, and as Jack approached he saw what Skuli was staring at. An opening in the ice.

Jack knelt beside him and looked down.

The hole was maybe a metre across. Inside was a kind of tunnel with an ice slope slanted like a giant slide, downwards and out of sight. Skuli pointed to where footholds had already been gouged for climbing down. Jack saw the same sort of set-up used by rock climbers: a thick red rope down one side of the slope, the top end looped through a metal peg fixed in the granite.

"I put the rope there," said Skuli. He got a head torch from his pocket and fixed it on. "I told you – I've been up here loads." He took another head torch out and handed it to Jack. "You'll need this. Watch me first." Skuli held the rope with two hands and began to climb down.

"Hang on!"

But Skuli was already a way below him. His eyes glinted up at Jack from inside. One hand still holding the rope, he crouched against the ice wall, straightening one leg, and then the other so he was sitting. Then, with a slight sideways grin back at Jack, he let go of the rope and slid away out of sight.

Jack gasped. The rope wobbled, limp. He twisted on his head torch and stared down into the hole. There was no sign of Skuli. Jack's chest squeezed tight. He must have fallen. Misjudged it. Maybe the ice gave way. . .

"Come on!" Skuli's muffled voice echoed up.

"The idiot!" Jack muttered. He hesitated, then took hold of the rope. *What am I doing?* Breathing hard, he gripped the rope in both hands and pressed a foot into the first toe-hole.

Hand over hand he climbed down. The gaps were well spaced and just the right size for the front of his foot to hinge into. Ice crystals reflected back the yellow beam of his head torch. He reached the place where Skuli had sat down. He waited a few seconds to get his nerve, then took a breath and eased himself round, keeping his heels pressed tight into the footholds. Then he slowly straightened one leg. . .

Jack looked down. Big mistake! He still couldn't see the end of the ice tunnel, even with the torch beam shining right into it.

"*Skuli!*"

Troll Boy Skuli, a voice inside him taunted. *Skuli Isaksen is half troll! That's why he likes being under the ground. . .*

"I've had enough of this!" Jack swung himself round to climb back up, but realized too late that he was sliding forward. He let out a stifled cry and clawed at the glassy surface, desperate to get a hold on the ice he hated. . .

But it was too late. He was travelling downwards, gathering pace through the tunnel, slipping faster and faster over the ice. Over and through and under.

3

ICE CAVE

Bark of rivers
and roof of the wave
and destruction of the doomed.
THE ICELANDIC RUNE POEM

Fast and faster went Jack, a human bobsleigh propelled by the slip of the ice. The cold took his breath away so he couldn't even scream. Light from his head torch skimmed the curved, racing tunnel; shadows flapped round like inky wings. Then the head torch was ripped off, plunging him into darkness. Icy spray stung his eyes as he fought and failed to find any kind of grip. He careered downwards, his face pulled taut by the speed, his body braced for impact.

There was a bump in the ice. Jack was flung up into the air and landed with a thud. The surface under him levelled and he slowed, finally spinning to a stop in a pitch black nothing.

Gradually his blinking eyes adjusted to the gloom. He had landed on his knees on a solid, cold surface. Light leaked from the tunnel he'd slid through, and there were thin shafts of sunlight from scattered openings in the roof.

He gazed at the enormous icicles hanging in jagged clusters, realizing that he was in some kind of cave. Columns sprouted from the floor, their glassy rounded tops glinting. There were strange sculptures everywhere: folds of blue ice streaked with pearly bubbles and silver veins; large blocks like tombstones jutting up from the cave floor.

Jack scrambled to his feet. *I'm under the ice.* He hugged his arms tight round his chest.

"You OK?" Skuli was by him, holding his arm to help him up. "Here's your torch."

"You could have warned me," Jack muttered.

"Sorry."

There were noises; creaking, dripping sounds that vibrated eerily around the chamber. A drop struck Jack's cheek and ran down his collar.

"Not far now," said Skuli. He trod off, weaving between the buckled ice statues.

"It's cold." Jack's voice echoed off the ice walls as he followed. He struggled to control his breathing. *Pressure compacts the ice and turns it blue...* The words reeled through his head, over and over, forcing him on. *Ice can stay in a glacier for more than a thousand years...*

Skuli had stopped and was crouched in the half-light. His breath formed swirling clouds as he spoke, making the space between them seem smaller.

"He's here," he said.

"What do you mean *he*?" Jack took a step forward. Then

he stopped. Gaped. All his other thoughts, his fear of the ice and the cold, forgotten.

There was a boy. Slumped against a wall of ice.

Dead.

4
DEAD BOY

The cave stood near the sea,
protected by secret spells.

BEOWULF

Jack stared at the dead boy in front of him.

He was wearing woollen trousers and a knee-length tunic with long sleeves. Round him was a thick cloak trimmed with animal fur, fastened on one shoulder with a brooch. He wore a helmet with a strip of metal over his nose, and there was a thick blond braid of hair down each side of the face.

Jack edged nearer, studying his face. The skin was a waxy grey-blue, speckled with ice. A scar on his forehead. The mouth bulged a little, swollen. And the eyes were open, staring back as if any second he might move and talk. But the most unnerving thing was. . .

"See what I mean?" Skuli hissed.

Shock rippled through Jack's body. It was like looking at himself in a mirror, but knowing the person staring back wasn't him. The same-shaped face; the same green eyes. It was like looking at his twin.

Jack's hand reached out towards the boy, then drew back, fingers tingling, as if there'd been a faint crackle of static in the air.

Skuli flapped his arms about wildly. "It's spooky. I thought he was *you* at first. That you'd got trapped down here." He crouched next to Jack. "That's where the arrowhead was." He pointed at one of the boy's hands propped against the ice, the fingers spread and hooked around an empty hollow. When Jack peered closer, he saw a dark patch on the palm, the same shape as the arrowhead.

Jack struggled with his disbelief. "But how did he get here?"

"Well, his leg looks pretty messed up." Skuli clenched his teeth. "Look at the funny angle – the bone's virtually coming out from the skin."

Jack stared at the boy's twisted leg; the jagged tear through the trousers; the bloodstains.

A loud creaking above them made them glance up. Melt water dripped on Jack's forehead. But his eyes were soon drawn back to the body. "He was probably dead as soon as he hit the ground," he said, feeling comforted by the idea. Otherwise what? A slow, agonizing death down here all alone? That didn't bear thinking about.

Skuli shook his head. "No. He was alive. For a bit anyway."

Jack's raised voice echoed round the cave. "And how can you know that?!"

"He had time," said Skuli quietly. "To write a message."

"Write *what*?" said Jack, his voice catching.

29

Skuli directed his torch at the ice wall behind the body. "That."

Jack's mouth fell open. There were grooves etched in the ice. Lines too regular to have been formed naturally. Lines like the ones he'd seen on the arrowhead. The boy's raised hand was right where the last one petered out.

"Runes!" Skuli said in an excited whisper. "I've no idea what they say though." He took a tattered notepad from a pocket and flipped it open. Jack saw symbols scribbled in biro. "I copied them all in here."

There was a sharp creaking sound and they both looked up, Skuli's forehead creasing into a frown. Jack noticed how buckled the walls were; there were cracks big enough to slide his hand into.

The echoes and the strangeness of the chamber were getting to him again. He kicked the heel of his trainer into the frozen ground, but couldn't feel his toes. The wind was wailing down the icy gullies and channels, and shadows flapped round them.

He found himself being drawn closer to the body. It had to be hundreds and hundreds of years old but still looked so fresh. What did all this mean – the arrowhead, the runes? The crazy coincidence of him and this boy looking so alike? He stared into the green eyes, and the boy stared back, and before he realized what he was doing, he reached out a hand. . .

Visions sparked through Jack's mind. He saw the boy, hunched, holding the arrowhead, carving runes into a wall of white. Then time seemed to spin back and he saw the boy hanging from an ice cliff, a man's face looking down at him.

Time spun back even further and Jack felt his eyes roll like he was passing out. There were fleeting images of trees falling, houses smashing, people running. . .

And then, through rising flames, there was that same man's face, leaping in the trembling air.

He heard the warning shriek of birds.

The face had been fleeting, but the look burnt into Jack's memory as he fell. The man's cruel sneer. His scarred lips.

And then, nothing.

5

THE WARNING
IN THE RUNES

A thousand winters they waited there.
For all that heritage huge, that gold. . .
was bound by a spell.

BEOWULF

Jack opened his eyes and blinked, slowly focusing on Skuli's
pale face. His body was cramped up. His back was freezing.
He felt at his head with a trembling hand.

Skuli gave him a worried smile. "It was like you were
having a fit or something. You all right?"

Jack tasted blood in his mouth. He must have bitten his
tongue. He let Skuli help him up.

But the touch of the boy's hand. . . What Jack had seen. . .
He swallowed. It was impossible, of course. He must have been
hallucinating. Something to do with the lack of oxygen down
here, or weird gases released from the ice. There was bound to
be something about it in one of Mum's medical books.

"He's called Tor." The words tumbled out before Jack
could stop them. *Don't be crazy!* How could he know

something like that? But it was there in his head; something he knew without hesitation. Like he'd always known.

"Tor," repeated Skuli, and there was a light in his eyes, as if reflected by something metallic.

"I froze to death," said Jack.

"What?"

"I mean. . ." *Why* had he said that? Early-stage hypothermia, probably, or the result of a bang to the head.

"He fell," said Jack slowly. "There was someone after him. Someone who wanted the arrowhead."

Skuli stared at him. "How do you know?"

"I saw him. . ." Jack struggled. "It was like. . ." How was this going to sound? Jack took a deep breath. He tried to find the right words.

"It was like I *was* him."

Skuli must think he was insane. He wouldn't blame him if he did. But he didn't show it, just nodded slowly and held Jack's arm to steady his shaking.

They gazed at the body and the marks on the ice wall.

"He used the arrowhead," said Jack. "He must have been going through hell, what with his leg. . ." He stopped and peered at the runes. It was as if the lines were coming into focus from far away; unchanged on the wall in front of him, but changing in his mind. Being sorted into meaning.

He traced over the first ones with a finger.

"*Beware this cursed arrowhead*," he muttered.

Skuli looked at him, wide-eyed. "You can *read* them?"

Jack snatched his hand back. "Course not!"

He could, though. He stood there, his thoughts bubbling with confusion, the cold biting into him and making it hard to think. He knew what the runes said. The same way he'd known the boy's name. No explanation. No question. He just knew.

Skuli eyed Jack closely. "What do they say then?" His dark hair flopped into his big trusting eyes.

Jack shook his head.

"Jack," said Skuli quietly. "So something weird's happening. We don't understand it, and we're scared by it. . . But you have to go on. Read them."

Jack bit his lip. He looked at the runes and let his breathing even out; a special bold power that felt good. Again there was that coming into focus; that sorting into meaning, until the runes and what they said were fused, one and the same.

"*Beware this cursed arrowhead.*"

Jack traced over more letters. "*Beware the four plagues.*"

He heard Skuli catch his breath. "*Four plagues!*" he cut in. "Just like in my grandma's poem! Go on!"

Jack's concentration was slipping. "*Seek another way to send the arrowhead back.*" His energy seemed to be draining away as he studied the runes. He picked out a string of letters and sounded it out. "*ís dahl. Ice Valley.*"

"Isdal! People *have* lived here since Viking times," said Skuli. He tried to laugh. "But this warning – it's from hundreds of years ago. We can't be in any danger now."

There was another creaking sound from above, and Jack was sure he felt the ground tremble. A cluster of icicles quivered and then went still.

Skuli swallowed. "What do those say?" He pointed to a line of runes higher up. "Tor made the lines much deeper," he said breathlessly. "You see that?"

Jack strained to make the letters out. "I can't exactly translate them . . . but I know what they're for. Protection."

Protection from what? This is crazy!

"You mean, a kind of magic?" Skuli said.

"No, not magic." Jack struggled to find the right word. *This is real life, not Harry Potter.* "Something ancient . . . from far back."

"Well, if they're protection runes, Jack," said Skuli slowly, "we're in trouble. 'Cos they're melting."

It was true. There was a wet gloss across the runes, and water dribbled down from them. How could they be *melting*? It was so cold in here; well below zero. Jack eyed a crack that ran right up the wall.

Something tugged at his memory. He fumbled to take the arrowhead out of his pocket. The metal was still warm; the heat prickled his cold skin. He squinted at the runes engraved around the edge, then held it up next to the protection runes. Water immediately trickled down the ice wall, erasing parts of the letters below.

"Some of those protection runes are the same as the runes on the arrowhead!" Skuli lowered his voice to a whisper. "They must be extra important. What do they say?"

Jack's head ached. The runes were blurry now; he was only able to read fragments. He stared hard at the arrowhead and tried again, and at last he had it. "*Air. Water. Earth. Fire.*"

Skuli stared at him, then recited hesitantly:

"*The death gold brings four deadly plagues:*
Air, Water, Earth and Fire.
The gold it must be buried deep,
Or else will life expire."

A horrible panic clawed at Jack. A panic he couldn't explain. He sprang at Skuli. "When did you take the arrowhead out of the cave?"

"What?" Skuli stuttered. "I don't remember exactly, but—"

"You have to tell me – *when*!"

"Only yesterday!"

"We have to put it back!"

Jack grabbed the dead boy's hand and pressed the arrowhead into the raw wound on the palm, trying to close the rigid fingers round it, trying. But there was a strange resistance, like two north poles on magnets repelling, gold and skin swerving apart as he tried to push them together.

Too late. Whispers flapped inside his head. *Too late.*

"Can't." Jack stood there with the arrowhead, panting. *Curse. Plagues. Death. . .* His head throbbed.

"Can't?" Skuli's eyes were round.

Get a grip, Jack! He put the arrowhead back in his pocket. "Why haven't you told anyone about all this, Skuli?" He viciously snapped an icicle and threw it down so it smashed. "People should know. Archaeologists or whoever."

"I know, I should have," Skuli said. "But you don't disturb someone's grave, do you? And once people know about this place, that'll be it. We'll never be allowed back in here!"

Jack gazed at the Viking boy, and the boy gazed back, his eyes like pieces of green glass. His throat tightened as he thought about how Tor had died with nobody to help him.

He had a fleeting image of his dad, walking towards the frozen lake. . .

He closed his eyes and turned away from the body. "I've got to get out." He started back the way they'd come, zigzagging between the warped columns and jagged slabs of ice. Was it his imagination, or were those cracks in the wall spreading?

"But, Jack, what if it's true?" Skuli was following behind. "What if there *is* a curse? What if the town's in danger? I took the arrowhead – so I'd be to blame!"

Jack reached the tunnel they'd slid down and grabbed at the glassy surface, trying to get a hold. Above was an oval of powder-blue sky. *How were they going to climb back up there?*

Skuli appeared at his side. "You keep this." He pushed the notepad containing the runes into Jack's hand. "See if you can read more later."

Jack shoved the pad into his pocket with the arrowhead. "Let's get out," he said, his voice louder than he'd intended in the echoey cave.

Skuli fished around and lifted up an end of red rope. "It's the same one we used to climb down. It goes all the way along the tunnel. Hold the rope and put your feet in the holes, see?"

"Thank god." Jack looked up the long white slope to the gap of sky. Fleetingly, a dark bird flew across it.

"*Friend or foe, the daemon birds?*" muttered Skuli absentmindedly. "I took the arrowhead, Jack!" he said again. "I have to make things right!"

There was the distant groan of shifting ice, making the tunnel vibrate. "Worry about that later." Jack grabbed the rope and climbed, jamming the tips of his boots into the footholds.

"Promise you'll help me!" Skuli called from behind.

"I promise! Now, come *on*!"

Jack pulled himself up the shaft, gritting his teeth with the effort. Skuli's voice spiralled up to him in a white cloud. "A promise can't be broken."

Jack kept climbing. If only promises were that simple.

I'll always be here for you, Jack, his dad had said once.

Jack struggled up the last few metres, then heaved himself gasping from the hole, before reaching to help Skuli.

And as they climbed down the rocks and away from the glacier, Jack was filled with a strange kind of ache. Like a part of him was still there in the cave, buried and trapped and waiting, underneath the ice.

6

SOMETHING
IN THE AIR

*There were exceptional flashes of lightning, and fiery
dragons were seen flying the air.*

ANGLO-SAXON CHRONICLES, AD 793

"Evening, warrior." Gramps saluted with a butter knife as
Jack came into the *kafé*, a warm cave smelling of hot coffee
and freshly baked cakes.

"Jack, love!" his gran called, balancing on a chair to pin
a coloured paper chain to the wall. It wobbled in the misty
draught from the door as Jack banged it shut. There was
a bark and a scuffling of claws on the wooden floor and a
white shape bounded forward.

"Sno! Come here, boy!" Jack held out his hand to his dog,
ready for the usual welcome of licks and paws scrambling
against his knees. But Sno stopped suddenly. He just stood
there all hunched up in the middle of the floor, his husky fur
bristled. Then he let out a low growl and slunk under a table.

"Sno?" Jack clicked his fingers, but the dog stayed put.

What had got into him? Instinctively Jack's hand went to his pocket. He felt the arrowhead there, heavy and warm.

"And, *hello*, holidays!" said Gran, getting off the chair. "Not that it feels anything like midsummer!" She gave an exaggerated shiver and threw a piece of wood into the stove. "Sit down, love, and I'll fetch you something before customers arrive."

"How's Mum been today?" asked Jack quickly.

"She's been doing her pottery all day," said Gran, getting out a plate. "She's sleeping, so I wouldn't disturb her just now, my sweet."

Jack went to sit at a table by the window. He watched Skuli cross the murky street and disappear down the steps to his house. In his mind he saw his friend's worried face. "*I have to put it right. Promise me, Jack. Promise you'll help me.*"

The sky was strangely dark. At this time of year, this far north, it was light nearly all the time. Even at night it never properly went black, just a deep shade of blue until the sun rose again. But now towers of cloud were building as though a storm was coming. Whatever they decided to do next, thought Jack, it was going to have to wait until morning.

"Nasty things, schools, Jack!" said Gramps with a wink. "Follow my advice and bunk off at every opportunity!"

"So he can turn out like *you*, Gramps?" said Gran as she put a steaming plate of waffles in front of Jack. "Not a good idea!"

Gramps blew her a kiss, then flicked on the wall telly with the remote while Gran went back to the counter to

40

serve some people who'd just come in, talking and laughing loudly.

Jack picked at the corner of his waffles. A gust of wind rattled the glass and the lights flickered a moment. *A plague of air.*

He shook his head. He couldn't help thinking about the things he'd seen when he touched the body in the cave. Tor carving the runes. Tor hanging from the ice cliff, that sneering face looking down.

The sky flickered with sheet lightning; thunderless, rainless. Jack's reflection looked back at him from the glass. It was as if Tor was there, looking in at him.

Jack stared at the telly and tried to push out his worries, listening to the tourist video Gramps had set to spool between programmes. He'd heard it a thousand times before. "*Isdal. Town of the Midnight Sun.*"

The screen filled with local landscapes as the smooth, soothing tones of the voiceover rang out, first in Norwegian and then in English. Gramps had been proud of that touch.

"*Isdal. Where there's always a friendly face. . . An ancient coastal town set in timelessness. . . A jewel between mountain and sea. . . A town shrouded in fascinating history and fantastical myth. . .*"

Jack knew all the words, in both languages. That's how sad *he* was!

"*Two thousand metres above the town, the rugged* Brennbjerg *peak stands watch over Isdal's sheltered bay . . . and on its rocky slopes, the majestic Isdal glacier, descending in close proximity to the town."*

There was an aerial view of the glacier, pitted with blue crevasses.

Tor. Jack thought of the cracks snaking up the ice round his body. The cave could collapse; then they'd never get him out. He had to tell someone, surely!

"Isdal's location close to the Arctic Circle means that on one very special day every year the sun does not set, and the whole town takes to the streets in age-old celebration, the Festival of the Midnight Sun. . ."

There was a shot of the sun, sitting on the sea's horizon like a fat egg yolk. People paraded the streets dressed in Viking helmets and long tunics, and danced round a bonfire, gold masks covering their eyes. Fireworks exploded across the sky. A Viking longboat was being launched into the bay, its dragon's head decorated with evergreen branches and flowers.

With a flurry of icy air, the *kafé* door swung open and a man came in, his windswept hair standing up from his scalp. "Evening, everyone!" He beamed, all teeth and red cheeks and thick glasses. Then he hurried across the room and settled down at Gramps's table, nodding at Jack as he took off his coat and patted down his hair into neat, slick lines.

Petter Alver; the head of Isdal Museum.

Just tell Petter, Jack told himself. *Let him do the rest. The bloke will be falling over himself to get to the glacier.*

So what was stopping him from telling?

Petter laughed out loud at a joke of Gramps's, pulling

Jack out of his brooding. He watched Petter wipe his eyes on a handkerchief. He could ask him about Skuli's ballad at least; he was bound to have heard it. Then maybe Jack could work out its connection with the ice cave runes.

Jack waited until Gramps had gone off to help Gran behind the counter and then went over to Petter's table. They exchanged a few words, about school, the weather, then Jack slipped in his question, writing a few lines on a paper napkin.

The death gold brings four deadly plagues:
Air, Water, Earth and Fire,
The gold it must be buried deep

"Ah, yes!" exclaimed Petter, snatching up the napkin before Jack could finish and adding the last line in his own scrawly handwriting.

Or else will life expire.

He adjusted his glasses. "I'm very familiar with this ballad, Jack. It dates back to Viking times, did you know that? Must be over a thousand years old. You may also know that my postdoctoral thesis was on Viking Isdal." He gave a happy little laugh. "My life's work, you could say! I led the team involved in the excavation of the Norse longboat found by our fjord here. It's a priceless national artefact!"

You've only told me that seventeen times, thought Jack. But he set his face into an "I'm impressed" look.

"Now, the ballad, yes." Petter squinted at the napkin. "There have been different scholarly interpretations, but the *gold* obviously refers to the sun. *Death gold* means sunset and the Arctic winter; and the idea of *burying the gold deep* refers to the disappearance of the sun necessary for its rebirth; the natural life cycle, so to speak."

Jack imagined pulling the arrowhead from his pocket with a flourish – *ta-da!* – just to see the look on Petter's face. *Interpret that, mate!* But he just sat there and nodded.

"*Air, water, earth and fire* – well, these are the ancient elemental forces, once believed to be the basis for all living things. It's not at all clear why they might be referred to as *plagues* though.

"There *is* evidence that a disease plague of some kind struck the town around a thousand years ago."

Jack felt his heartbeat quicken as Petter went on excitedly.

"From excavated burials we can deduce that a good portion of the town's population was wiped out. Perhaps that's what is being referred to.

"As an interesting aside, there is evidence that sacrificial hangings were a favourite way for Vikings to worship the main Norse god, Odin. Keep any such plagues at bay, if you will."

A cold draught circled the table, blowing the napkin to the floor. Sno gave a low growl as it brushed his paws.

Petter drew closer. "Between you and me, Jack." His eyes glinted. "Between you and me, I'd give anything to be able to speak with a person from back then. To *really* understand how they thought and felt, you know?"

He gave a short, wild-sounding laugh and for a single, sickening moment, his mouth twisted into a sneer and it wasn't Petter's face Jack saw; it was the face of that other man – the one Jack had seen when he'd first touched Tor. . .

Jack shrank back and Petter's eyebrows raised a little, his expression back to normal. "Why the sudden interest in the ballad anyway, Jack?"

"Well," he stammered, struggling to make sense of what he'd just seen; trying to remember his prepared answer. "My mum was telling me she learnt the ballad when she was young and . . . you know, she's, well, hard to get through to sometimes."

"Ah, I understand." Petter's face relaxed into a sympathetic smile. "You're trying to show an interest; get her to *come out of herself*, eh?"

Jack nodded shakily, getting up from the table. "Thanks for your help, Petter."

Jack went back to his seat and took a bite of waffle. It was like chewing cold rubber. Had he imagined Petter's look? He dangled the rest of the food in Sno's direction, but the dog stayed under the far table, curled in a tight ball, watching him.

The logs on the stove crackled and flared and Jack's skin tingled with heat. He peered out of the window at the deserted street. From across the room, he heard Sno growling deep in his throat and saw the dog's thick fur tremble.

"*. . .the mighty Isdal glacier. . .*" droned the telly. The image quivered, static distorting the picture.

The lights flickered and Gramps looked up, cursing under his breath. He changed channel. A football match appeared on-screen. News stories spooled fuzzily along the bottom. *Scientists monitor unusual tectonic plate shifts. . .*

Jack's phone buzzed. *Vinnie.* But the message took ages to come up and letters of the text were corrupted.

FRE3ZING T* DE#TH? S@ME STO&Y H3RE M%TE

The footie match now looked as if it were being played in the middle of a blizzard, and the sound was gone. Gramps swore again, getting a tea-towel-in-the-face reaction from Gran. He stood on a chair to fiddle with the wires at the back of the telly.

Petter lowered the book he'd been reading. "Maybe it's because of the *You-Know-What*s!" He winked. Jack eyed him suspiciously, but there was no sign of the scary weirdness he'd seen before.

"What's that?" said Gran, retrieving her tea towel.

Petter gave a chuckle. "Didn't your husband tell you?" He started laughing as if it was the funniest thing ever. "What he told us last night in the bar?"

"OK, Petter," said Gramps. "We don't need to repeat all the details. An electric cable needed repairing, that's all."

"Thought you said it was a real mess-up there, up on the Pass."

"First I've heard of it," Gran said, bringing a cup and

plate. "What's this about the Pass?"

"It's all repaired now, my sweet." Gramps gave the telly a hefty thump. The sound was back, but a thick fuzzy line now spooled up the screen. Jack heard the words *my lousy job . . . electricity board*, and lots of swear words, but muttered this time so Gran wouldn't hear.

"I can't believe he hasn't told you. . ." Petter widened his eyes and let out a fake cackle. "About the *demon birds*!"

Jack flinched. *Friend or foe, the demon birds. . .* Wasn't that what Skuli had said?

"Just like in our ballad, Jack!" said Petter, as if he'd heard Jack's thoughts. He mimed drinking from a glass, waggling a finger in Gramps's direction.

"Yes, thank you, Petter," said Gramps. "Thanks for that. Most grateful."

"You said it couldn't have been any *ordinary* kind of bird," Petter continued to mock. "Enormous feathers everywhere, nothing like you'd ever seen!"

"They *were*!" Gramps fiddled with the ketchup bottle on the table. "A whole lot of big black raven feathers and nothing else." He cleared his throat. "Just a larger-than-average bird getting electrocuted, I suppose."

"That's *not* what you said last night!" grinned Petter.

"Really?" Gramps took a noisy slurp of coffee. "Well, it's amazing how a few beers can liven up a story."

"You said it looked like the birds had clawed through the cables!" Petter snorted. "Can you imagine? They cut corners on maintenance, then try to blame a bird!"

Jack's skin flushed with heat again. "*Could* a bird do that,

47

Gramps?" he asked quickly.

"No chance in hell!" said Gramps. "Any normal animal would be dead as soon as it even *touched* a cable of that voltage."

"Which is why your gramps got a bit spooked by the whole thing, I dare say!" smirked Petter.

Gramps shook the creases out of his newspaper so the pages shivered. *BIZARRE WEATHER SET TO CONTINUE*, said the headline. "As I said, the power is restored, as good as new!"

Just then the lights flickered again. Petter let out a loud laugh.

Skuli's words came back to Jack. *Something weird's happening. We don't understand it. . .*

He felt Skuli's notepad in his pocket. He should be trying to read more of the runes, not sitting in here eating waffles!

There were movements outside, children in the street looking in. Noses pressed up against the glass. Fingertips pointed at the pastries, leaving grubby marks. Any minute the *kafé* would be full.

He had to try and understand those runes. But not here.

Saying goodnight to Gran and Gramps, Jack took his jacket and slipped out the back way with Sno skulking behind at a distance, passing through the yard and up the wooden steps to his bedroom.

Reaching his door, he paused and turned. Out of the corner of his eye, he had seen someone, lingering at the bottom of the steps. He peered hard into the gloomy twilight, but there was nobody there, only trails of mist creeping along the street, lingering in the branches of the huge twisted pine tree in the middle of the square. A faint light spilled up from the chink of below-street window of Skuli's basement flat. The breeze nipped at Jack's face and he shivered.

Jack coaxed Sno inside then shut the door. He tried the light switch, but it was dead. He lit the candle in a holder by his bed and closed the curtains. Sno crouched on the floor, looking up at him, ears pressed flat against his head. Jack took a breath, and then pulled Skuli's notepad from his pocket.

7

THE VISITOR

At the gates of death, I wake thee.
THE INCANTATION OF GROA

Jack lay on his bed and opened the notepad. He turned a page, and then another, scanning the runes, his fingers flicking through more and more impatiently. He couldn't read any of it. It was just a load of lines that made no sense.

He thumped his pillow. The bond he'd felt with Tor had been so real. He *had* to understand what it all meant!

Sno pushed his head through the curtains and hooked his paws on to the window ledge. His ears were pressed forward; his body taut and still.

Jack got up and went over to the window. He moved the curtain and looked out. Mist swirled round the doorways in wisps, rising into little towers of white like ghostly figures, then sinking and spreading between the shuttered wooden buildings. Beyond the houses he could see Brennbjerg mountain, a humped mass in the lingering blue twilight. The room momentarily flashed violet and there was a crack of thunder. The tiered roofs of the church on the hill flickered bright in the lightning, the slanted wood tiles glinting like scales. In one place a cross was illuminated, in another, the open mouth of a dragon. By the tower, a tangled Isdal flag flapped like a grotesque bird impaled on a pole.

What *was* the arrowhead anyway? Jack thought. Where had it come from? He reached a hand into his pocket and touched the warm metal. Sno let out a low growl, and the candle flame jumped and shrank, hissing on its wick, and the shadows twitched on the walls. Jack eased the arrowhead out of his pocket.

Sno snarled, and then lurched, snapping at Jack's hand, making the arrowhead spin on to the floor.

The shock of it took Jack by surprise and he instinctively hit back, a hard blow to Sno's muzzle, and the dog crouched, baring his teeth.

"You *bit* me!" Jack grabbed Sno's collar and pulled him to the door. "Don't you *ever* bite me again! *Out!*"

Jack slammed the door shut. He heard Sno scratching on the wood and whimpering a while, and then everything went quiet.

His hand trembled as he sat on his bed and inspected the teeth marks in his hand. Sno had never done anything like that before, not even when he was a puppy playing. Blood pooled in the two puncture marks on his palm, near the place where the arrowhead had cut him when Skuli first

51

handed it over. But there was no sign of that cut, none at all. He turned his hand over in disbelief, scanning the skin. The wound had been there that afternoon, quite deep, but there was absolutely no trace of it.

Jack swallowed. Skuli had said something about that, hadn't he? About where the arrowhead had cut *him*. *It healed super fast.*

Sno was nervous of the arrowhead, that's what it was. Could Jack blame him? Animals sensed stuff. He went quickly to the door and opened it. "Sno! Sno!" But the wind battered back his voice, and there was no sign of his dog.

A bird landed on the electricity cable overhead, a dark silhouette against the sky, its shape magnified as lightning threw its shadow on to the wall. It looked weird, clamped on the line like that as it swung violently from side to side. The thunder cracked overhead. Then, one by one, in an unbroken ripple, the lamps went off all the way down the street.

With a shudder, Jack went back inside and shut the door and bolted it. He crouched to look at the arrowhead where it was lying on the floor. *Air, Water, Earth, Fire* its runes said. There was a flurry of wind like sharp stones thrown against the glass and Jack scooped the arrowhead back into his pocket and eased the curtains apart, peering through the gap.

Another gust slapped the window, rattling the pane. The church bell struck and Jack counted the strokes: seven . . . eight . . . nine . . . ten.

He thought about Tor, alone in the ice. Then Skuli, alone in his house.

With his finger he wrote in the layer of condensation: *Beware this cursed arrowhead. . .*

He stopped with a gasp and moved back from the glass.

There were the letters, clear as anything. Only they weren't the letters he'd intended to write. Without even realizing it, he had *written in runes!*

That meant. . . It had to, didn't it? He scrambled to get the notepad and pulled it open, almost ripping a page in his hurry. He hunched over the runes, and there was that familiar coming into focus; that sorting into meaning. . . *Beware this cursed arrowhead. Beware the four plagues.*

He gave a shocked laugh, of excited panic. The message was coming strongly and impatiently into his mind, as if this was his chance and he mustn't waste it. He grabbed a pen and scribbled as he read:

"Seek another way to send the arrowhead back. Flames over water. A midnight sun."

The runes were ended. He had done it. But what did all this mean? He had to go and tell Skuli right away. The words tumbled round his head as he shoved the notepad in his pocket and made for the door. *Flames over water. . . Midnight sun. . .*

There was a sudden bang and a crack, and a rush of freezing air, blowing out the candle flame. The window swung loose from its latch and slammed against the wall. A framed photo on the windowsill was swept to the floor and the glass smashed.

Jack rushed over to retrieve the picture and force the window shut. He wiped the silver slithers of glass from the surface of the photo. Him and his dad bundled up in hats and football scarves, their faces fixed in stupid grins. Their last-ever weekend together.

We all still want to know how it could have happened. . . Gran's words came back to him. *But we have to be practical now.*

Practical Jack. That's what his dad used to call him when they did jobs around the farm: fixing the tractor; putting fencing round the lake. . .

He smoothed the photo and propped it back on the windowsill.

And that's when he saw the figure.

Someone across the street, half hidden in mist and shadow. Jack pressed his face close to the glass and peered down, his breath fogging the pane. Whoever it was, they were looking straight at him.

There was lightning and the growl of thunder; then more lightning filled the room. Dark. Light. And with each flash, the shape came closer. Jack shrank away, but still the figure came nearer, rising until it was level with the first-floor room. Jack gave a cry and stumbled backwards, but it was already at the window and runes were rapidly being drawn in the fog on the pane. . .

Then the figure was in the room.

At the foot of the bed.

Jack pressed himself against the wall. He gaped in terror, his stomach twisting with recognition.

Tor.

Standing silent. Expressionless.

Pinning Jack with his empty gaze.

Tor raised one hand, slowly, as if it was a painful gesture. He uncurled his fingers and held up his palm, and Jack cried out as he saw the blackened outline of rotted flesh; the shape of the arrowhead scorched deep into the skin.

And then Tor was retreating. Fading through the wood of the closed door, leaving only a faint, lingering whisper in Jack's head. *THE TRUTH.*

The truth about what? Jack rushed to the window and saw Tor down in the street, moving slowly away, but stopping briefly to look up at him.

THE TRUTH, said the runes on the windowpane. The words turned over and over in Jack's mind as he pulled on his jacket. His hands shook so much that he was hardly able to do up the zip. He found his woolly hat and a head torch, flung open the door and rushed down the steps, headlong into the gusting wind.

8

THE STANDING STONE

And shadowy creatures came gliding forth . . .
night darkening over all.

BEOWULF

Just keep up, thought Jack. *Keep your nerve.*

The wind blew hard in his face, making his eyes water and turning the dark street into a blur. Tor moved ahead, never slowing down, sometimes seeming to drift over the ground rather than walk on it; sometimes merging with the wooden buildings he passed. Thin clouds swept fast across the ash-blue sky. A dark shape came hurtling down; a roof tile, smashing on the pavement. Jack flinched but did not stop.

He found himself climbing the winding lane up the hill towards the church. Behind him the waves slapped the boulders on the shore of the bay, and, turning, he saw water spray up on to the buildings closest to the sea wall.

On he went. Now Tor was at the church, moving between the headstones of the graveyard. Jack followed, twisting between the angels and scrolls and stone skulls.

Tor's pace became more urgent. The wind caught at his outline, pulling it into wispy threads. Now and then he disappeared altogether, before reappearing further away. Jack struggled to keep up.

Tor reached the cluster of spindly trees at the far end of the graveyard, the same way Skuli had taken Jack to the glacier. Jack pushed his way through the dense, sharp branches. The leaves shivered as the wind hissed through them. He felt his way along the overgrown wall. He was out of breath and hot, despite the cold air. He got to the rusty gate with its bars and spikes, and found it swinging open.

He went through, twisting to avoid the thorny stems, and there was Tor, one hand resting on the overgrown standing stone, his back to Jack, totally still.

With a sharp intake of breath, Jack stopped. Slowly Tor turned to look at him. Jack couldn't take his eyes off the Viking boy's face: its closeness to his own, its shifting transparent sheen. . .

Tor mouthed something, and although no sound came out, Jack heard the words in his mind, sounding out in a heavy, halting way, as if with great effort and pain. . .

It has begun.

Send the arrowhead back. . . Save Isdal.

Rescue me from the ice.

And as Jack watched, Tor's face was changing, rippling like the broken surface of a lake, shifting and fading. . .

Beware – my – brother.

And then he was opening his mouth wider, wider, and

Jack shrank back, staring at the bloody stub where Tor's tongue should have been.

And then he was gone.

Jack stumbled to his knees. "Tor?" His voice rang out into the empty air. He got up and staggered in a circle, looking in every direction. "Tor?"

But Tor was gone, leaving only that same faint, lingering whisper.

The truth. The truth.

The words pulsed through Jack's head. Why had Tor led him here? Heart pounding, he stepped towards the standing stone. He rubbed at a patch of lichens and pulled twists of old ivy. He put on his head torch and let the light spill over the murky surface as he tugged and scraped at the centuries-old crust. His fingers were going numb through his gloves. He tried to hack the layers off with a stone, but the ancient moss was dried on, set like cement.

Jack remembered the arrowhead.

He took out the blade and reached up to slice into the pitted surface near the top. The arrowhead glinted. The skin of moss and lichens came away easily, uncovering the stone below.

And then he saw.

Carvings.

He continued with the arrowhead. At the tip of the standing stone – the unmistakeable shape of the Brennbjerg mountain appeared, but with vast forests stretching round its base where there were buildings now.

"Isdal," Jack muttered. "From the past."

Houses dotted the shore of the bay, and instead of fishing boats, there were boats with dragon heads: longboats; the kind the Vikings had.

He found runes and ran his fingers along their grooves, able to read them. . .

AIR.

More carvings, etched into the stone.

A tree being ripped out by its roots. People fighting to stay upright in the wind; arms raised; mouths gaping in horrified circles. A woman falling from a house. A man lying dead under a toppled tree.

WATER.

Jack scraped more quickly.

Lashing rain. Surging waves. Smashed boats. Smashed houses. People swept away. Half-rotted bodies, washed from their graves.

EARTH.

People running. Crushed by falling rocks. Swallowed by great cracks.

Air. Water. Earth. . . Jack sat back on his heels, breathing hard, trying to take in what he was seeing. Had all this terrible stuff really happened? Or was it all just some made-up story; some far-fetched myth?

He ran the arrowhead across the stone again. More runes appeared. Lines and lines of them. He read aloud, his voice faltering.

"The survivors of the Great Plagues raise this stone in memory of their dead kin.

"Njáll Halldórsson. . . Hermundr Njállsson. . . Geira

Eiríksdottir. . ."

The arrowhead peeled away the coating and more names; Jack struggling to read them as the meanings of the runes began to blur. . .

"Rannveig Koðránsdottir. . . Manni Anundsson. . . Otkatla Mannisdottir. . ."

Dozens of them. The names morphing back into incomprehensible runes as he scanned over them. A list of the dead, like you got on war memorials.

Jack swallowed. The standing stone was a memorial stone.

Realization hit.

Centuries ago the plagues had already struck Isdal. Hadn't Petter said as much? *A thousand years ago . . . a good portion of the town's population was wiped out.*

Tor had shown him as well, hadn't he – the first time Jack had touched him? Those fleeting images of trees falling, houses smashing, people running. Tor had been there; he'd seen the plagues happen!

Jack hesitated, then scratched fast at the last area of stone.

FIRE, said the runes; and underneath. . . The razor-sharp gold started to take off the surface of the stone itself. *What kind of gold did that?* But no matter how much Jack scoured, there were no pictures. Nothing.

Jack put the arrowhead shakily away and ran his hand over the blank surface. The town hadn't been *totally* wiped out. He knew that much. The last plague had been stopped somehow, before everyone was killed. But *how?*

Jack scrutinized the standing stone again. There was

something else he noticed now. He peered closer.

In each scene there were extra figures in the background; people with weapons; clubs and axes. Even children. They seemed to be attacking each other. There were bodies on the ground, being trampled. Bodies hanging from trees.

But why would people start hurting each other in the middle of the plagues?

The wind tugged at Jack's jacket. He remembered the way the kids had treated Skuli. Lukas with that rock.

It has begun.

Save Isdal.

Faint thoughts filtered into his head; ones that weren't his own. He stood very still, forcing his anxious mind to relax, letting the thoughts come; past latching on to present. The truth that Tor had brought him here to show.

The plagues were going to happen again.

Just like they had before.

Jack's chest tightened as he looked at the people falling, drowning, being crushed; then at the uncarved section of the standing stone, ominously empty.

He had to get to Skuli!

Send the arrowhead back.

He scrambled out of the gate, through the tangled trees and back through the graveyard with its grimacing stone skulls. The church bell struck, echoing, grating clangs. Birds cawed harshly to each other.

Jack sensed a movement in the bushes close to him, and he skidded to a stop. A pair of eyes stared out.

"Sno! Come here, boy!"

Jack shoved one hand in his pocket and caged his fingers round the arrowhead. "It's OK." He crouched and held out his other hand. "It's still me, boy. I'm still your Jack."

Slowly, with more coaxing, the dog edged forward, eventually allowing Jack to stroke his muzzle; and with a small, nervous whimper from Sno, the two of them ran on together.

The church bell struck three . . . four . . . five. . . Jack stumbled on the loose gravel of the lane, dodging between the gateposts and on to the main street.

Send the arrowhead back.

Back where? Not to the ice cave. He'd already tried that. Besides, the glacier was melting fast. That wasn't a solution. It'd only be a matter of time before the gold got washed out, wherever they put it. No, back in the ice – that wasn't an option.

Flames over water. A midnight sun. What did that mean? There was only one day a year when Isdal got the midnight sun. The summer solstice. And that was tomorrow night. But the rest?

Rescue me from the ice.

That part of Tor's message had been clear enough. The first thing was to get him out. Out of an ice cave that could collapse any time.

Jack sprinted down the street as the church bell rang on: eight . . . nine . . . ten.

Jack got to Skuli's and went down the steps to the door in one jump.

"Skuli!" he called, slapping the door with his palm.

No reply.

"Skuli!" He banged the door with his fist.

A line of light appeared along the bottom of the door, which swung open a crack. Skuli, fully dressed, bleary-eyed, peered out. "Jack?"

"Let me in!" Jack pushed his way past Skuli and closed the door. He found himself in a kind of hallway with more stairs beyond, leading down. "We have to get Tor's body out of the cave before it collapses!" he said. "Right now!"

Skuli's eyes widened.

"I saw Tor!" blurted Jack. "He led me to a standing stone by the graveyard. The plagues happened in Isdal before – and they're going to happen again!"

Skuli stood there in the hallway, wobbling slightly, his face suddenly very pale.

"I'll tell you more on the way. You know mountain rescue stuff, right?" said Jack. "We have to get Tor out, that's all I know for sure."

Skuli's eyes were huge with amazement. He nodded slowly, then started pulling on his boots. "We'll need equipment," he said, his fingers trembling as he tied his laces. "It won't be easy. Tor's metres down."

Jack reached for the door handle and glanced at his watch. "Seven minutes past ten." His mind whirred. "What do we need? Rope. . ."

"Ice axes and crampons," said Skuli, zipping up his jacket. "And a body stretcher – you know, the kind rescue teams use. Dad keeps everything in our big shed round the back."

"Let's go then."

Skuli grabbed his coat from its hook. "I remembered where Gran's book is," he said, tugging at the sleeves. "The one with the ballad in it." He started back down the stairs. "It might tell us. . ."

Jack held Skuli's arm. "Never mind that now!" He thought about the cracks in the cave and the melting ice. "We need to get going!" He pulled open the door and they stepped out into the night.

"We can do this, Jack, can't we?" Skuli's voice rang over the gusting wind, thrilled and hopeful.

"I promised you, didn't I? That I'd help you put things right?"

We're getting Tor out. The enormity of it pressed at Jack's chest; the weight of what they had to do. But there were prickles of excitement mixed in with the dread.

We're getting you out, Tor.

If only the ice would hold till then.

THE ANCIENT
BALLAD OF ISDAL

In ancient times in a far-off land
Where battles were lost and won,
The Norse gods gathered in a mighty hall
And our story is begun.

A glowing hall protected by
A flawless roof of gold,
Leaves of gleaming arrowheads,
A glory to behold.

But in this hall of warriors
One held a traitor's mark,
And from the roof a gold leaf stole
And escaped o'er Bifrost's arc.

How the gods in the hall lament
Thief and arrowhead.
The great god Odin, fury filled,
Cursed Midgard where he'd fled.

And so four deadly plagues were sent,
Air, Water, Earth and Fire.
And the gold it must be buried deep,
Else will all life expire.

Oh Yggdrasil, oh tree of life
Your first leaf it did fall,
The winter of the gods began
In Valhalla's holy hall.

And Ragnorak will come at last
And end the Norse gods' reign,
And all the leaves of Yggdrasil
Will fall as golden rain.

So will the arrowhead bring four plagues
And feed men's worst desires,
For by plague fire can the gold return
To Asgard's hallowed shire.

But a single other way there is
To set the cursed gold free:
On a death boat under midnight sun,
Through the toil of warriors three.

There surely be another way
To send the arrowhead home.
Carried by warrior true of heart
On a blazing death boat lone.

When fire, air, water, earth unite
In the light of a midnight sun,
The curse is broke; the gold is freed,
The evil is undone.

Daemon birds, a spell shall weave
To. . .

Excerpt
TENTH CENTURY, ORIGIN UNKNOWN

Trouble is coming to the man who . . .
loads himself with pledges.

HABAKKUK 2:6

PART 2
THE
PLAGUES

N

9
BACK TO THE GLACIER

And Tor did fall to his icy doom,
and the traitor thus was smashed.

THE SAGA OF VEKELL

Jack and Skuli hurried along the street, carrying the equipment on their backs. Patches of mist lingered round the houses, and stretched in viscous strands towards the church on its hilltop with its gape-mouthed dragons. The Brennbjerg mountain rose up beyond, huge and brooding against the blue-steel sky, trapping the town against the sea. Hidden from view, somewhere ahead of them, Jack felt the presence of the glacier, melting and cracking.

The wind was stronger now. It came in hard gusts. Bins have been overturned, and rubbish came swirling past, making Sno snap and bark. A white shirt pulled off a washing line swept by them like a ghost.

"The plague of air," said Skuli, his rucksack bulging on his back. His teeth chattered. "This is the start of it, Jack, isn't it?"

Jack clawed at his shoulder where a loop of the body stretcher was rubbing. If this wind got much worse it was bound to make the cave more unstable. To stop himself thinking about it, he ran through the equipment list in his head. *One collapsible body stretcher. An extra coil of rope. Two ice axes. Two pairs of spiky crampons for the bottom of their boots. A harness. Two head torches. Two pairs of thick leather gloves. . .*

On Church Lane, the bunting had ripped loose and twitched like whips overhead. All that was left of the Festival poster on the lamppost was a ragged corner and the words *GO BACK*.

"Got the arrowhead safe?" Skuli asked, and Jack put a hand to his chest pocket, feeling the gold over his heart: a dead weight, surprisingly heavy for such a small object.

Doubt pricked at Jack. "Do you think we're strong enough to pull Tor out?"

"It'll need the both of us," called Skuli. "We'll use a belay system with the rope that's already there. Figure-of-eight rethread knots. There's a granite rock we can use as our anchor point."

Jack nodded, clueless. He just had to hope it all made sense when they got there.

They reached the graveyard. Sharp twigs rained down on them from the battered trees and grit flew up from the path and stung Jack's eyes. As they pushed the secret gate, the wind slammed it shut on them. They rammed it hard with their shoulders to get it open.

Skuli stopped to stare at the standing stone, at the stark

images of the plagues, but Jack pulled at his rucksack to urge him on, remembering Tor's words. *Rescue me from the ice.*

The wind was fiercer the more they climbed, slapping gusts that made their eyes water and slowed them right down. Small rocks showered down from the surrounding slopes. They stopped talking; it took all Jack's concentration just to keep on the track without being pushed to the edge. Sno followed, head down, his fur ruffling into spikes.

Jack heard the muffled church bells strike midnight, the clangs almost drowned out by the air wailing between the rocks. Already dawn was coming. He looked up at the strange sky, the clouds in lines like dark rib bones, dawn light glowing coldly between them.

He turned off his torch. Tonight the sun only went down for a short time, and tomorrow night it wouldn't go down at all, just sit on the horizon before rising again – and whatever it was they had to do would have to be done by then.

The path wound higher, and their boots spat stones as they scrambled up the slope. Had that been a movement above them? Jack peered nervously, but saw nothing. Sheets of lightning flashed between the clouds, and thunder growled ominously under the screech of the wind.

They got to the banks of the melt river where the track flattened and widened, and they tried to pick up speed.

"We'll need to send the stretcher through the ice tunnel," shouted Jack.

Skuli nodded. "Then slide down ourselves and strap Tor

on," he called back. "But once he's out, where will we hide him?"

"By the standing stone somewhere?"

There was no vegetation now, only rock. The melt river flowed faster, tumbling and crashing. The air was sharp with cold, and every step was an effort, struggling against the wind.

Then they turned a bend and there it was. Towering up ahead, the glacier with its cracked blue face and gashes of grey dirt. Jack looked at the shimmering ice, so still in the stormy blue night, as if waiting. This moment might have been a thousand years ago as easily as now.

"That doesn't look good," said Skuli. There was a web of fresh cracks across the front of the glacier. It seemed to be melting faster than ever, despite the biting wind.

Jack looked at the ice and shuddered; then he dipped under the safety barrier. "Let's get the stretcher to the hole."

They climbed the tumble of rocks up towards the granite platform. Jack followed Skuli, pausing to wait for tiny lulls in the wind to heave himself up, then pressed close to the rocks to wait as the wind snapped at his back, trying to tug him down. Sno circled and barked below.

They arrived, panting, at the hole and its slanting tunnel, the fractured glacier looming over them.

Jack slipped the stretcher off his back and watched Skuli open it out and click it into place to make a rigid frame. Immediately the wind caught the stretcher underneath and lifted it off the ground. Jack had to spring forward and lie along it to keep it from being blown away.

A fist-sized lump of ice tumbled from higher up the glacier, sprinkling them with shards. Jack heard Sno howl.

Skuli didn't look happy. "It should be just *me* who takes the risk!" he said. "It was me who took the arrowhead, not you!"

"Skuli—"

"You might not get out."

Jack held his arm. Tried to smile. "I'll be OK." But the smile felt like a crack in his face. "It'll need the both of us to get Tor on to the stretcher and carry him through the cave."

Skuli bit his lip, then nodded. Jack helped him push the stretcher into the hole and it disappeared over the edge and slid away.

Jack made to go next, but then he stopped.

Skuli looked at him. "Shall I go first?"

Jack shook his head. "Give me a second."

Get going, Jack Tomassen. It's only ice. There's no time.

The pegged red rope was writhing in the wind. Jack grabbed hold of it. He took a long, deep breath as if he was a swimmer about to go under water.

Then he took a step. Down. Back down into the icy hole.

10

INTO THE ABYSS

It is whirled from the vault of heaven... and
then melts into water.
THE ANGLO-SAXON RUNIC POEM

Hurry, Jack told himself as he crossed the ice cave, the empty body stretcher balanced on one shoulder. He heard Skuli's quick breathing behind him as they dodged round frozen columns and overhead icicles. *Get Tor, then get out fast.*

He gazed up at the fractures in the roof, wider now, scattering thick rods of murky light across the cave. He could still hear the wind, clawing at the cracks as if it was something alive, trying to find a way in. And everywhere around him was the sighing of the ice, and the relentless drip of melting. Thin, fast trickles of water slipped over the walls, like veins over blue flesh. His heart rattled against his ribs. He felt the cave pressing round him like a prison. *Hurry. Hurry.*

They reached Tor, and Jack knelt by the slumped body, laying the stretcher flat. He looked into the face so like his own. His fingers hovered by Tor's arm, but when he touched him this time there were no visions, only a strong ripple of emotion. Danger. Fear.

Skuli crouched near the stretcher, wiping water off his face. "Tighten the straps like this," he demonstrated. "Then check the tension."

Jack nodded and together they opened the bright orange straps wide, getting ready to lay the body on the stretcher.

With the push of the glacier over hundreds of years, how come the cave hadn't broken apart before now? Jack wondered as he tugged at a strap. It had to be because of the protection runes. He glanced up at their melting smears. Soon there wouldn't be anything left of them.

Skuli took a firm hold of Tor's legs. "Ready?"

Jack clasped the arms, cradled Tor's head against his chest.

"One, two, *three*!"

Then Tor was inside the stretcher and they were fastening the straps, pulling them tight and getting ready to lift.

Jack went first, gasping with the effort. He held his end of the stretcher behind him, picking a careful, looping route back to the tunnel. He found the rucksack they'd left there, and the blood-red rope dangling down.

All around them was an ominous creaking, like the strain on the hull of some huge ship slowly breaking apart on rocks.

"Put the stretcher down," Skuli panted. He tied the loose end of the rope to the head end of the stretcher and tugged the knot tight. "It'll be much more slippy going up this time. Remember how much faster we came down?" He looked grim. "Did you feel those places where the tunnel's cracking?" He took the ice axes and crampons out of the rucksack and helped Jack tie the metal spikes to the bottom of his boots. "Hold the axe as you're climbing, and if you feel yourself sliding you can whack it into the slope and get a better hold. I'll go first to show you."

Jack stepped up into the footholds after Skuli, one hand on the rope, one holding the axe, his sharp crampons holding him against the slick surface. The wind wailed above and cold air spiralled down at him. Loose flakes of frost drifted into his eyes from the sides of Skuli's boots.

Jack saw the hole ahead and its gap of sky. After a while he saw Skuli hoisting himself out. He urged himself towards the hole, but here the tunnel was buckled, with cracks running over the surface, and his legs twisted awkwardly as he tried to find a grip. He had a stabbing memory of the lake on their farm back in Northumberland. White trees. Dark birds against a blue sky. His dad's face under broken ice.

With a short cry, Jack heaved himself up. At last the wind pulled at his hair, and as his head surfaced the force of it made him gulp for breath.

He scrambled out of the hole and saw Skuli at work with the red rope, untying it from the metal peg. Jack helped him fight the wind to heave some of the slack and knot a section round Skuli's hips. The air was alive, whipping their voices away as soon as they spoke.

"Need an anchor point," Skuli mouthed and tied the end of the rope round a jutting rock, securing it with another tight knot. He fitted a pair of leather gloves over his wool ones and gestured to Jack to do the same, showing him where to hold the rope. "Braced stance!" he shouted, and the two of them sat on the edge of the hole, legs bent and heels dug into rocky clefts.

And they pulled. Hand over hand, taking the rope in, together in one fluid movement. Jack felt the tension in the rope; the friction between the ice and the stretcher. He imagined Tor edging his way up the sloping tunnel.

The wind was savage. It came at them in bites. Jack's eyes streamed with cold. But they were bringing Tor out!

But then he began to worry. *What if they hadn't strapped the body tightly enough? What if the tunnel cracked on the way up? Would they be able to hold the full weight of the stretcher? What if the line snagged or snapped?* Jack watched the red rope slide over the icy granite. He willed the stretcher upwards. Stared intently down the gloomy tunnel. . .

Yes! The bright orange top of the stretcher came into view. "Nearly," Jack yelled. "Keep it going!" The stretcher shifted towards them. He saw Tor's body strain against the straps. . . It edged higher. . . And then it stopped.

Jack looked at Skuli in alarm. They tightened their grip and heaved, but no matter how hard they pulled, it wouldn't budge. Skuli pointed a finger and Jack saw the rope above the stretcher was wedged in a crack of ice a couple of metres below them.

"Can you climb down the footholds and free it?" Skuli shouted anxiously near his ear. "Use the axe. I've got to keep on the main line. Here's the harness. I'll tie you on the spare rope just in case."

In case of what? Jack got his legs through the harness and Skuli attached the extra rope, looping it across himself then knotting the other end round a second anchor rock. He crouched back in position and gave Jack a nod, and Jack stepped backwards into the footholds.

He got to the stuck bit of rope and thumped at the hard cleft of ice that was trapping it. But the rope only sank deeper. He tried kicking. He eased round and chipped at the ice with his axe. *Don't cut the rope,* he told himself. *Whatever you do, Jack Tomassen, don't do that.*

He saw Skuli looking down at him, hunched in the brunt of the wind. He tightened his clammy fingers on the handle of the axe and brought it down hard. Sharp silver shards flew at his face. A piece of the rope came free. He hit again, then again, and the rest of it twanged loose.

"Pull!" Jack yelled, giving the thumbs up. Skuli's face creased with effort. The stretcher inched higher, so close now that Jack could touch the top edge with his boot. "Yes!" he hollered, starting to climb back up to the mouth of the hole. "I'm coming to help!"

And that's when Jack saw them. Two birds falling across the gap of sky, their wings closed tight, their claws stretched. And as he was stopped, paused those few seconds to stare, he heard it. A noise like tearing metal that set his teeth on edge.

The air was suddenly very still. The ravens shrieked and circled closer.

A cracking thud detonated somewhere under Jack's feet, and the sloping ground of the tunnel he'd been about to step on to gave way. Instinctively he struck out with the ice axe, leaping sideways, hooking the curved wall. The blade wedged there and he clung to its handle. His feet scrambled desperately for a hold, finding only the thinnest of ledges to balance on. A chunk of rock hurtled past and a smashing sound came from a long way down.

Jack's chest was pressed against ice, his pulse roaring in his ears. He turned his head round and down to see – eyes wide – the tumbled tunnel and the stretcher dangling freely over a plummeting abyss.

"Jack!" gasped Skuli. His face was a glaze of sweat as the rope and the anchor took the strain. "Climb up. Use the axe. I'll hold your rope."

But if I fall, thought Jack, *will Skuli be able to hold both me and the stretcher?*

"Tor first!" Jack yelled. "*Go on!*"

The stretcher juddered up, painfully slowly. Jack saw the muscles in Skuli's neck bulge with effort. How he was managing it alone, Jack didn't know. Up past Jack came Tor, his staring green eyes meeting Jack's . . . up to the lip of the hole. Jack caught his breath. Out. . .

Tor
was
out.

Jack's chest shuddered. He shuffled a foot experimentally on the ledge. It seemed to be solid. He tightened the loop of the ice axe round his wrist, his next movements unfolding in slow motion in his head. He moved his foot again, managed to kick a toe-hole, managed a step up. He eased the axe from the ice and got ready for another small step. . .

The ice exploded under him.

Jack pitched forward, driving hard with the axe, the air spinning and splintering. He saw the powdery snow round the blade flaking and tearing and coming away. He gripped the handle in his clenched fist but his hand was slipping. His feet kicked for a hold but there was none. Only empty space.

. . .And he was falling, falling like Tor had fallen, plunging and spinning, the cold stripping away his breath.

Rushing ice and rushing air, then something hard against his head.

Then, nothing.

Tor grips the front of the boat, stares across the heaving waves from the dragon's head. He reaches a hand up the carved neck, feeling the cross-shaped split in the dragon's eye.

Another hand catches him hard on the side of the face. "Ready to prove yourself, little brother?"

Vekell is by his ear, a mocking lilt in his voice. Excitement too. Tor feels it rippling through the group of men waiting on the deck. Dawn light catches their swords; the gleam of their metal helmets; their small smiles of anticipation.

Vekell strikes him again, harder this time. "Warriors never show weakness, remember that." Tor can smell the sickly sweetness of mead on his breath. "You are the son of a chief. You will do honour to your clan or I'll cut out your tongue!"

Tor studies his proud brother. The tunic edged with emerald snakes, the rich earth colours of his fur cloak, and the domed helmet inlaid with snarling, bright silver wolves. Plaits tied with strings of sharp animal teeth. He's used to his threats.

Tor nods and turns away. His eyes search the twilight; the coastline rising and falling through the ebbing mist. He scoops up the ship's cat and strokes its bristling fur. He'll show Vekell! How proud his father will be with the gold he is going to bring back. It is bound to lift him from his sickness.

Tor thinks of the victory feasts he has been to. The treasures and stories the men returned with. He feels a pang of sadness. If only his father could be here with them now.

A shape appears on the blurred headland. Tor cranes forward, feeling his heartbeat quicken. A great stone building. A flower-shaped window glows with a pale light. A tower with turrets like horns. Dark birds circling. Tor hears the closeness of the men's breathing. Their urge to kill.

Unarmed coward monks, thinks Tor. With their puny one-god worship. They'd deserve everything they got.

Wouldn't they?

The boat approaches the shore noiselessly through the dark water and advances until the sand holds it. One of the men sends down the heavy iron anchor, unhooking it from its snake-shaped clasp, and its chain grates across the deck. The men surge forward, but Vekell stops them with a raised hand. There is a murmur of angry questions.

Tor hears Vekell mutter. "Something not right."

But the men are impatient. "New plan of attack?" one growls.

Vekell looks a little longer, then shakes his head. He drops his fist like a stone and the men splash down into the water and spill across the beach. Swiftly they stream up and over the low cliff and Tor follows, stumbling in his haste. His palms slap the freezing water. There is the stench of seaweed. Shells crush under his boots. He scrambles up a slippery gash in the cliff.

A burial ground. Tor runs through it, twisting past the grey stone slabs and strange winged figures. A coarse cry cuts the air. A scream. The sound of metal on metal. More screams.

I'm missing out! Tor thinks. Hurry. Hurry.

Sounds of smashing. Shapes flit past columned doorways. *Which way?* The mist is thick here. Heavy as a death shroud.

Tor holds up his axe. He runs through a gloomy courtyard and dips under a doorway engraved with skulls.

He slows to a stop. The hall is deserted. The thick stone walls muffle the yells and screams from outside.

Tables and stools stand in rows. Along one side are painted wood statues the size of real men. Shafts of dawn light make reddish patches on the floor. Tor hears a bell clang a warning.

He holds his axe tight. There is a movement at the far end of the hall. A pool of candlelight. A lone monk crouched over a table.

Tor slowly draws his sword. Throat dry, he steps nearer. The monk is writing slowly with a feather quill, mumbling under his breath. Now and again he dips the nib into a small clay pot. His fingertips are stained black with ink. He seems oblivious to what is going on outside.

Tor creeps closer, strangely fascinated by the beauty of his work, by the elegant lines of lettering edged all round with silver leaf. By the way the candle catches gold, blue, bright red. . . He shakes himself and raises his sword to strike. . .

The wick of the candle spits and the monk looks up at him. Their eyes lock. Tor hesitates.

The monk springs up. Before he can react, Tor feels a blow of full force on his face and is knocked back.

The man has a sword. He makes deft slashes through the air. The point slices Tor's forehead and he tastes blood. *Monks don't fight back!* His axe is slammed from his hand. His sword crashes down on the stone floor, a ragged stub.

Tor turns and runs, the monk close behind. Out of a side door on to the open meadow. All around him, men are fighting. Dying. One of his clan staggers past, a dark red line across his back; another is knocked to his knees and an axe blade hacks down at his skull. A monk's chest is sliced open. A Norse man writhes, impaled on the spike of a crucifix.

Vekell? Where is my brother? Monks don't fight back!

Gasping, Tor runs on, half blinded, the bleeding crust tightening over his face. The sky is streaked with red and against it he sees a tower, a narrow cylinder of stone, set apart from the monastery. Two birds circling.

He is at the base of a tower. Has he lost the monk? He darts through the door. Rushes down the spiral steps.

Down?

But it is too late to think of dead ends.

Down and down and down. . .

11
AFTERMATH

The good sons... on the gallows hang.
THE LAY OF HAMDIR

Cold air stung Jack's face. He felt himself floating. He opened his eyes . . . and looked straight down into the plunging chasm.

His feet thrashed in panic, but there was nothing except air between him and the harness and the jagged collapse of ice far below. The rope creaked, turning him in a slow circle like a hanged man. He struggled for breath as the blur of images sparked through his mind again. Tor . . . the monastery. . .

"*Jack?*" He strained towards Skuli's shouts, but saw only a bulging wall of ice, the rope running over it like a trickle of blood. He imagined Skuli on the edge of the granite platform, exhausted after pulling out Tor. The strap of the ice axe bit into his wrist. He swallowed hard and heard his own voice fierce in his head. "*Get to the wall and climb!*"

Jack tightened his grip on the axe handle. He kicked his legs to get a movement in the rope, then jolted his body to increase the sway. As he came close to the wall he swiped his boots forward and, with a grunt, drove their spiky crampons at the ice. Again. Again.

Finally he got a toe-hold. He lashed out with the axe in one hand, hoisting himself up the rope, stepping jerkily up the cliff. Agonizingly slow. His muscles formed fiery knots. Needles of pain shunted through his legs and arms.

He rounded the overhang and – so close – saw Skuli reaching down over the edge. Jack strained an arm towards him and their fingertips brushed.

"More!" gasped Skuli, his face shining with sweat.

Their fingers locked together and Jack swung himself up. He slithered on to the granite platform, panting, and Skuli gripped him with a laugh, wiping away grubby tears. Jack smiled back weakly. His whole body hurt. He couldn't speak. He just wanted to lie there. Lie there and rest, jaw against stone, looking at Tor.

Not a hair on Jack's head stirred. There was even a bit of sun on his face.

Skuli rummaged in the rucksack and they nibbled on chocolate bars and sipped at cartons of juice.

"I hate ice!" said Jack. He picked up a lump and threw it feebly, smashing it against the platform and spraying them in tinkling shards.

Skuli gave a snort, and then the two of them lay there, screeching with hysterics.

"It's not funny!" said Jack, laughing and wincing. He wiped his eyes. "We did it, Skuli," he said, feeling a warmth going through him. He touched his forehead experimentally, getting flakes of dried blood on his fingertips.

"Got a nasty cut there." Skuli gave him a sideways grin and nodded towards the body stretcher. "Now you look even more like Tor."

Tor. Jack sighed. *We got you out.*

Then he shivered. He'd seen Tor's memories. Now he knew exactly how he had got that scar.

"I think you were knocked out a while," said Skuli.

Jack scrambled to his feet. "How long for?"

"Twenty minutes, maybe more. . ."

Jack tugged at his sleeve to see his watch. "That long?" *Three ten a.m.* "And you were trying to pull me all that time? In that gale and everything?"

"The wind stopped," said Skuli. He pulled off his gloves and inspected the sores on his hands. "It was weird. Almost exactly when Tor was pulled out. Like someone flipped a switch."

The plague of air. Scenes from the standing stone came tumbling into Jack's mind. The screaming people. The crushed man. How much damage might the windstorm have done to Isdal? What about Mum and Gran and Gramps?

And Sno! What about Sno? "We have to go down!" gasped Jack, limping over to the stretcher. "Hide Tor by the standing stone, then check what's happened in town."

Skuli caught his mood and hurried to attach another rope system to the stretcher, and they lowered it over the rocks to river level.

Jack saw now that a whole section of the glacier had collapsed. A huge shaft of ice had split and fallen from the face into the jumble of vast slabs below. The ice cave was completely buried.

The stretcher touched the coarse gravel of the river edge and slid to a stop, and Jack and Skuli clambered down after it.

Jack saw Sno wriggle out from a rocky alcove and bound towards them, barking. He leapt up at Jack, whining and licking at his face, then did the same to Skuli as they each got hold of an end of the stretcher.

"Good, boy. It's all right. *Lift, Skuli!*"

Jack tried to concentrate on the path, carry the stretcher without stumbling. But his heart was pounding. Tor's words kept coming back to him: *Beware my brother. Beware my brother.* He had the uncomfortable idea that they were bringing a lot more than just Tor down from the mountain with them.

"Look at *that!*" said Skuli.

From their vantage point Jack could see the Pass road, the only way out of Isdal, blocked with a collapsed pylon. In the distance, strange grey clouds were massing, lightning flickering through them in weirdly shifting colours.

They picked up speed. Skuli walked in silence; Jack too, worrying about his family. They made it to the standing stone and quickly laid Tor in the hollow behind it, covering him with the torn-off branches that were strewn all around them.

They ran back through the graveyard and down Church Lane. They dodged the debris covering the street: overturned bins and scattered rubbish; ripped-off roof planks and smashed glass. The bell tower struck once. *Half past four.* The sky was ominously dark, the sun obscured. Somewhere high up, Jack thought he glimpsed a dark bird.

As they got on the main street, he saw with surprise that the *kafé* was open. Through the window he saw a mass of people hunched around the tables, which were lit by candles.

"Sent the kids wild, the storm did!" Gran was saying as Jack and Skuli slipped in. "Dancing around in the wind they were. It's a miracle none of *them* were killed."

"Someone was killed?" Skuli asked.

The room went quiet. Only the droning crackle of the television: *Isdal. . . Where there's always a friendly face. . .* Everyone stared at Skuli like he was personally to blame. There were none of the usual smiles of welcome.

"Where have *you* been?" Gran snorted. "And you, Jack? Slept through it, did you? I'm the one who's had to keep this place open all night to take in hysterical people." She clattered a pile of plates into the sink. "Why I'm bothering, I don't know."

"But people have been killed, Gran?" asked Jack uneasily. He knew he must look a sight, but Gran seemed oblivious. Why was she acting like that? There was a horrible hostility in the air. Only Gramps looked confused by it.

Jack struggled to keep the panic from his voice. "Is Mum OK?"

Gramps nodded vaguely in his direction.

"At least three dead," said Gran matter-of-factly.

Jack stared. Gran seemed to have a sort of bluish tinge to her lips.

"A woman blown off her balcony," she said. "A man hit by a tree. . ."

Jack stared at Skuli. *Just like I saw on the standing stone.*

"One smashed skull," finished Gran with a satisfied flourish.

"Should have known better than to be outside in a gale," said Petter, the museum curator, slurping his coffee.

There were murmurs of agreement.

"Isdal's cut off," someone said. "No boats in or out till further notice. Sea's too rough. Aircraft grounded too. And the Pass is blocked. The bodies are being taken to the church until the coroner can get here."

Jack and Skuli crept close to the stove, Jack pinching a couple of warm hardboiled eggs from a bowl on the counter as they passed. They sat out of the way with Sno, eyeing the room.

"Everyone's going mental!" Skuli whispered, cracking an egg and peeling the shell.

"Look at their lips," Jack said in a low whisper. "Do you see it?"

Skuli gazed around with a frown, then nodded. "That blue colour? All of them have it. What's going on?"

Jack shook his head, eating his food. They had to keep

their nerve and work out what to do next; they only had until midnight. . . But a tiredness weighed him down. Gran tossed another log on the fire and the air throbbed with a harsh heat, making the cut on his head prickle. He saw Skuli's eyelids dropping closed.

Did something just go past the window? A dark shape swooping low past the glass?

"*A night of global terror. . .*" crackled the television.

Jack's eyes shot open and he elbowed Skuli awake. The pictures were a fuzzy mess; the words came out in snatches. "*Freak storms . . . thousands dead worldwide . . . emergency services stretched thin . . . reports of spreading violence. . .*" The telly died completely.

Petter cackled. "People *are* saying it's Ragnorak! The end of the world!"

Thousands dead? Breathing quickly, Jack pulled out his phone and tried to message Vinnie.

NO SIGNAL

He tried again.

NO SIGNAL

He gave Skuli a shaky smile. "I'm sure your dad'll be OK." But Skuli just frowned and didn't answer.

"Don't bother with the phone," Gramps growled at Jack. "The power's off. No signals. Gas pipe fractured. We only had electricity because of our emergency generator. It's like going back a thousand years in one night!"

Gran craned forward like a bird ready to peck. "Get more generators hooked up then, husband!" she snapped.

Petter sneezed and wiped his nose with a tissue. "Yes,

you'd better get things sorted out by midnight. We can't have the festival getting messed up by power cuts. There'll be hell to pay!"

"Three people are *dead*, Petter!" Gramps said. His speech was slurred slightly, as if he was fighting against himself to get the words out. "A festival's the least of our worries and the worries of the families."

"Better off out of it!" A blob of spit flew from Petter's mouth as he spoke. Candle smoke coiled over his head in a weird draught, making a grey wreath. "Two stupid old men and a good-for-nothing woman. They should have stayed indoors!"

Jack stared at Skuli in shock.

"People die all the time," said Gran savagely from the sink. She swung round with a soapy pan so that bubbles dripped down her arm and gathered at her elbow. "I lost my son in England. Went straight through the ice and drowned to death in freezing water. Get over it!"

Jack's chest tightened painfully and he saw Skuli pale and still. It couldn't be his real gran, talking like that, could it?

"The Festival of the Midnight Sun must go ahead!" insisted Petter. "No matter what! The tradition goes back centuries!"

Jack felt a dangerous tension stretching across the room. He felt the arrowhead in his chest pocket, heavy and warm.

"It's part of our heritage," Petter ranted on. "Our birthright!" He took another swig from his cup.

"That's *my* coffee!" A man sprang up and pulled Petter

to his feet by the collar, a twist of fury on his face. It reminded him of Lukas Brudvik, the raised rock in his fist. He remembered the standing stone; people hurting each other with clubs and axes. . .

The room went silent, watching. Nobody tried to step in. Jack saw Petter's fingers reach back and slowly tighten round the handle of a knife. . . "Odin's vengeance," he said, very quietly.

There was a movement outside. Black wings brushed the glass and seemed to spread over it. Claws scratched the pane. Two pairs of glinting eyes looked keenly in.

Like someone had flicked a switch, the man doubled over, coughing, releasing Petter from his grip. In an unnerving ripple effect, scowls fixed themselves on the faces of the other adults in the room, their shoulders slumping.

Jack stared round in alarm. He noticed sweat on the foreheads of his grandparents, their bloodshot eyes, their faces sagging pale and greyish. . . All the adults had it. They sat in subdued menace, then pulled themselves up and staggered out of the *kafé* like zombies, mumbling about feeling unwell and having to get home.

Gran and Gramps hardly protested when Jack and Skuli helped them out of the *kafé* and into their house next door, guiding them up the stairs to their room to lie down. "What's going on, Jack?"

Jack heard Skuli's voice wobble as they crouched tensely on the landing, listening to the fitful breathing of Gran and Gramps.

"Let's go to yours," said Jack. "Have a look at this ballad

you've been telling me about. See if it can give us any clues."

Skuli nodded.

"Just let me check on Mum first. I'll only be two minutes."

Skuli leant against the banister. "I'll wait here."

Jack slipped quietly up the second flight of stairs to Mum's pottery studio. "Mum?" he called quietly at the door.

No reply.

He pushed the door open and stepped in. Mum was lying on the sofa under a ruffled blanket. She was asleep and muttering. Her face was pale and there was clay on her cheek. Jack thought suddenly how fragile the murky light made her look, as if the shadows on her face were bruises. He spread the blanket over her.

"Mum," he said gently.

"Jack?" She reached towards the sound of his voice. He saw clay under her fingernails. "You were gone so long. . ." Her face creased with concern. "Oh, what did you do to your head, love?"

Then her eyes went wide, and she was staring past him, and Jack turned and saw what she was looking at.

They were all around him. Distorted clay sculptures. Lining the display shelves, in rows along the walls. Twisted shapes of people screaming; being crushed by trees, by rocks. . . Scenes from the plagues. . . Kids killing kids. . . A raven with its wings spread wide. . . A boy hanging from a tree by a rope. . .

"*Mum?*" Jack clenched his hands into balls. "Why did you—"

"We've no choice," Mum whispered. "It's our bloodline, Jack."

What did she mean "it's our bloodline"? Why had she made those horrible things?

His mum strained forward. Her forehead was clammy and she was breathing strangely. Her lips were tinged with blue as she spoke, quickly, eyes drifting. She drew herself towards him with a gasp and gripped him tight. "You can't escape your blood."

"What do you mean? Mum?" Her nails were digging right into his neck. "Mum!"

But she sank back against her pillow with a shudder. She closed her eyes and was back in a fitful sleep.

Jack covered her with the blanket again and stumbled out. Sno nuzzled his fingers as he went down the stairs in a daze with Skuli. Once outside he had to steady himself against the wall of his house.

Skuli held his arm. "Jack?"

But Jack shook his head, unable to explain. "Let's get to yours," he said, his jaw tight. "Look at the ballad."

They set off, seeing again those unearthly storm clouds to the north. Though there was no wind now, the clouds were moving quickly closer, as if swept along by some other force.

And they'd almost got to Skuli's when they were stopped in their tracks. Stopped in their tracks by a terrible scream.

12

CHILDREN MURDERERS BE

Here is our land sorely blemished. Here there are
murderers of kinsmen and killers of children.
SERMON OF THE WOLF TO THE ENGLISH, 1014

The thin, high-pitched wail came again, like someone being murdered.

"It's coming from the harbour." Jack pelted down the long stretch of steps that led towards the water, Skuli following. He could hear shouts now. Laughter. Another screech of pain.

Sno gave a sharp bark and the boys skidded to a stop at the bottom of the steps. Jack grabbed his collar and clipped on his lead, then held the dog's muzzle as they edged round a parked car, then Gran's van, and crouched behind one of the wooden buildings by the water's edge. Figures materialized from the mist only a little way in front of them – seven or eight kids on the pier, half hidden under hoods – and now they saw where the shrieks were coming from.

Lukas had a cat by the scruff of its neck – a grey scraggy thing. It twisted to get free, its legs thrashing, its paws swiping the air, its fur in stiff peaks. It hissed and scratched, but Lukas held it tight, hardly flinching. He started winding thick string round its legs as the other kids sniggered and jostled.

"Odin's vengeance!" one shouted.

Jack felt Skuli grip his shoulder. Weren't those the exact words Petter had used in the *kafé*?

Jack saw the girl from his class, Emma, hovering at the edge of the group, as if she was deciding whether to join in or not. He remembered how she'd tried to stop them hurting Skuli on the playground. But now she just stood there, saying nothing.

When the hands of children murderers be. The words of Skuli's ballad thudded into Jack's memory.

Three tiny kittens peered out from some nearby bushes, mewing.

Lukas pulled the cord tighter. The exhausted cat spat and gave a low, desperate growl. Its legs were bound tight. "Stray cats are vermin," Lukas announced. "They need hanging up!" And with one deft movement he wound the loose end round a post and hauled the cat in the air.

It swung there like a pendulum, eyes horribly wide. Lukas peered at it for a moment, as if surprised by what he'd done. Then he started laughing until the others joined in. He prodded it with a stick. Other kids started picking up sticks. Emma had one too.

Jack watched, stomach churning. Hardly thinking what he was doing, his hand curled around the arrowhead and lifted it out.

He felt Skuli hold his sleeve; saw his look of alarm.

Sno flattened himself against the ground with a growling rumbling whine and Jack quickly tied the lead through a wooden strut of the pier. "You stay here too, Skuli," he mouthed. "Be ready to run." He stepped forward, holding the arrowhead like a weapon, feeling the dangerous power of it in his hand.

The kids turned to look as Jack approached, sticks in hands. A strange quiet rippled through the group, the cat forgotten. All of them mesmerized by the light reflected off the arrowhead blade.

Jack's mouth was dry. He remembered yesterday in the woods, the way Lukas had been ready to slam that rock at his skull.

"I've come to cut the cat down," Jack said, as steadily as he could.

No reply. Nobody moved.

Light from the arrowhead played over Lukas's face. His mouth gaped open slightly, his blue lips making a circle.

"I've come to cut the cat down," Jack said again, more loudly. He went towards the animal, angling the blade to cut its bonds.

"You're dead, Tomassen," Lukas muttered, but kept his distance. "Dead like your daddy."

There were snorts of laughter. A burning sensation flared up in Jack's chest. *Don't react. Free the cat. Then get Skuli and Sno out. Get yourself out.*

Jack lifted the arrowhead to the cord and was through it instantly. The cat was strangely calm as he cradled it and sliced the remaining knots. He lowered the furry bundle to the ground. It stumbled up and then shot away into the bushes.

Jack straightened slowly, watching the kids all the time, pressing the arrowhead back into his pocket.

A little smile played on Lukas's lips. He took a wavering step closer.

The kids were spreading out, forming a circle round Jack and Skuli.

"We're going to leave now," said Jack evenly.

Lukas ignored him. "Yesterday you pushed me over, Jack Tomassen," he mocked. "You made me hurt myself." The other kids moved forward too, as if they were attached with invisible ropes. "It's vengeance time."

Then Lukas came at him with a cry; but it was Emma who sprang to try and grab the arrowhead first. Jack spun to one side and she screamed out as the blade slashed across her fingers. She crouched, cradling her hand as it gushed with blood.

Lukas lunged again. His skull slammed Jack's chest and knocked him backwards off the pier. Jack skidded along the stony ground, lacerating the skin along his leg. Blood from his opened-up head wound trickled into one eye. His ears buzzed with a chanting chorus. "Kill! Kill!"

He saw a fuzzy Sno going crazy, and Skuli crouched, fumbling to undo the lead.

Lukas grasped Jack's neck, lifting him and pinning him against the wooden planks of the boat shed, then he thudded his back against a window, shattering the glass.

The kids hooted. Only Emma stayed silent.

Now Lukas had him on the floor in a headlock. Jack punched, but Lukas tightened his grip, hitting Jack's jaw hard with his knuckles. He felt Lukas's fingers in his pocket, trying to wrestle the arrowhead out, grunting as it cut him.

No way! Jack wrenched up his knees with a shout and heaved his boots forward, knocking Lukas away.

But the boy was looming over Jack again in a moment, giving him a kick in the chest. Another kick to his side and Jack rolled across the ground, his lungs heaving. The heavy boot swung back for another go and Jack twisted with a yell to grab it, pulling as hard as he could. Lukas crashed down. The shouts grew louder.

Skuli gave up on untying Sno's lead. He charged at Lukas, but a kid sprang forward giving him a thump that sent him sprawling, and the mob of kids closed round like quicksand, pinning him to the ground.

"*Skuli!*" Jack struggled to get to his feet and help his friend, but kids were on his legs, his arms, a gritty shoe sole against his throat. He saw Emma, looking down at him, her hands limp at her sides.

"This isn't you," Jack wheezed at them. "Just let us go."

Lukas spat some blood on to the ground. He was smiling. He had hold of something. A queasy panic swirled in Jack's insides. It was a length of thick rope. Rope knotted in a noose.

"This isn't you, Lukas," Jack said again. "You have to stop."

There was the smallest pause, the tiniest flicker of hesitation in Lukas's face, then his eyes were glazed and hard again. He tugged the rope to test the tension. "Who first – you or the Troll?"

Jack's eyes searched the surrounding buildings desperately, the closed doors, the shuttered windows.

A voice rang out. A voice to make people listen. "Leave them alone."

Everyone stopped to look.

"Leave – Jack – and – Skuli – alone!" Emma shouted again.

A crisp packet skittered over the pebbles and into the water. Fat drops of rain peppered the surface like bullets.

"So, Tomassen," Lukas swapped the noose from one hand to the other, swaggering nearer. "Is Ugly Eagels your girlfriend now?"

"Stop this, Lukas," Jack said quietly. "This isn't—"

"I asked if Ugly Eagels was your girlfriend!" he spat.

"No," said Emma. "I'm *yours*!" And she rushed forward and kicked Lukas hard, sweeping his legs from under him, making him crash to the ground with a grunt.

"Run!" Jack grabbed Emma's outstretched hand and they dragged Skuli up from the kids' surprised, slack grips. With a swipe of the arrowhead he'd cut Sno free.

"Run!" Jack cried out. "*Run!*"

13

REFUGE

The wall on the outside is higher than a man, but . . .
he made it much deeper to prevent the eyes and
thoughts from wandering.
THE LIFE AND MIRACLES OF SAINT CUTHBERT, BEDE

"Lock the door! Bolt it! *Quick!* Get that chest of drawers across it!"

Jack, Emma and Skuli crouched in Skuli's basement flat, staring up at the thin rectangle of window at street level. Feet ran past. Stopped. They heard snatches of conversation through the glass. *My mum and dad are out of it. . . All the adults are. . . No one to boss us around. . . Do what we like!*

The kids ran on, feet slapping the puddles.

Why aren't we affected by the illness? wondered Jack. He touched his head, wincing. *Why aren't we acting like the other kids?*

Outside was murky like twilight, even though it was the middle of the day. But if it hadn't been for the weird darkness, he thought, they'd never have got away.

"Have they gone, do you think?" wheezed Skuli. His eyes were wide and scared in the gloom. He pulled down the blind and drew a heavy curtain across, then limped over to try the light switch. "Still no power." He lit three tall candles in holders round the room, and they sat on the sofa huddled close inside the triangle of light, listening to the sounds of lashing rain and dripping water.

Jack flexed his bruised fingers. He stared round Skuli's large sitting room, trying to block the fight from his mind. There was a gloomy corridor at the far end, a wide bench along the wall, tools hanging over it. "Got to sit tight a while longer, I reckon," he said huskily. "Get the ballad, Skuli."

"What's going on?" said Emma as Skuli scrambled up and started rummaging in a cupboard on the other side of the room. "What happened to me back there? What they did to that cat—" Her voice broke off.

Jack stroked Sno, burying his fingers in the soft, white fur. He and Skuli looked at each other.

"I could feel myself wanting to join in."

Emma bit her nails. "Getting cut, it kind of shocked me out of it." She turned her hand over, frowning. "It hardly shows up now."

Her face was pale as she looked up at Jack. "I heard kids talking. You and Skuli are at the top of some kind of hit list." She pushed her wet plait behind her back. "I'll be on it too now. Oh god! Those kids looked like they were really going to. . ."

"They were," said Jack. He saw Lukas again, with the rope, his thick fingers testing the tension in the noose. "But that's the least of our worries."

"It's like they've changed into other people," she whispered. "What's got into them?"

"We should tell her about the plagues, Jack," Skuli said, still searching the cupboard. "She needs to know everything if she's going to help us. She's not affected like the others. Look at her mouth. She doesn't have the . . . you know, the mark!"

"*Plagues?*" Emma touched at her face. "What are you two going on about?""

Jack gave a quick nod. He turned to Emma. Where did he start? He decided to plunge straight in.

"We found a dead boy."

Emma bit her lip. "The kids didn't . . . *kill* him, did they?"

"He was already dead," Skuli said from inside the cupboard. "Had been for quite some time."

"How long?"

"Just a thousand years or so," said Jack.

Emma let out a short laugh. Then her eyes widened as what he'd said registered.

He showed her the runes in Skuli's notepad. He told her about Tor and the arrowhead and the plagues; about the standing stone; his visions; how it was too late to put the arrowhead back.

"Oh god," Emma said quietly when he'd finished. "The Festival of the Midnight Sun. The longest day; the shortest night. The least evil time of the year. But that's midnight *tonight*!"

She was pacing in agitated excitement now. "And there were all those deaths on the news, did you see it? All caused by freak gales and stuff. It's not just happening here, it's spreading everywhere!"

"The world is always supposed to be ending," Jack said dryly. "Only this time it's for real."

"There must be someone who can help us," said Emma.

"Who?" said Jack. "All the adults are sick, and we're completely cut off."

They sat in silence, letting the reality sink in.

"Will my parents be OK?" said Emma, tugging at her plait.

"No," said Jack bluntly. "Nobody will be. Not unless we find a way to send the arrowhead back to wherever it came from."

"*Seek another way to send the arrowhead back,*" muttered Emma, reading from the notepad. "*Flames over water. A midnight sun.*"

"Found it," said Skuli, coming back with a book. The brown leather cover was hanging off and the front page tore as he tried to turn it. "You can still read most of it. There's lots of pictures with the verses in between." He tapped the first page. "*The Ancient Ballad of Isdal.*"

"Careful!" said Jack. "You'll put your finger through it!" He took the book and laid it gently across his knees, Emma and Skuli sitting either side and craning over his shoulder. "*Tenth Century,*" he read, heart thudding. "*Excerpt from. Origin unknown.*"

"In ancient times in a far-off land
Where battles were lost and won,
The Norse gods gathered in a mighty hall
And our story is begun.

A glowing hall protected by
A flawless roof of gold,
Leaves of gleaming arrowheads,
A glory to behold."

"That's Valhalla!" breathed Emma as they looked at the faded picture. "Where all Norse warriors were supposed to go if they died bravely in battle."

"See the gold arrowheads in the ceiling?" exclaimed Skuli.

Jack went on reading.

"But in this hall of warriors
One held a traitor's mark,
And from the roof a gold leaf stole
And escaped o'er Bifrost's arc.

"Weird," broke off Jack. "That's the second time the arrowheads have been called leaves."

He read on.

"How the gods in the hall lament

Thief and arrowhead,
The great god Odin fury filled
Cursed Midgard where he'd fled.

"And so four deadly plagues were sent,
Air, Water, Earth and Fire,
And the gold it must be buried deep
Else will all life expire."

Emma shivered and they huddled closer. "Those gales we had, and all the damage they did. . . And this rain that's started. . . What does the 'buried deep' part mean, do you think?"

"The arrowhead was buried in the ice cave," said Jack slowly. "Maybe that somehow trapped its power; stopped the plagues from starting."

"That fits," said Emma. "But, listen! If a way to trap the arrowhead's power is to bury it down deep, why can't we do that again? I know the glacier's melting, but why can't we find another place to put it?"

"How deep would it have to go?" Skuli twisted the sleeve of his coat. "The ground round here is pretty much solid rock once you start digging – it'd take way too long!"

Emma frowned. "I guess you're right. But there are *so many* golden arrowheads in Valhalla! Why would just *one* of them be so massively important to Odin?"

Jack tapped the next page of the ballad. "Listen to *this*. . .

"Oh Yggdrasil, oh tree of life

Your first leaf it did fall,
The winter of the gods began
In Valhalla's holy hall.

"Yggdrasil?" said Jack.

"Don't you get it?" said Skuli excitedly. "The Vikings thought there was this enormous tree, as big as the universe, with branches and roots stretching through nine different worlds. Asgard is the world where the gods are, and Midgard is where humans live."

"I know all that," said Jack. "But the ballad's saying that the arrowhead is one of the leaves of this tree thing, so—?"

"Yggdrasil's not just any old tree!" interrupted Emma. "It's the *tree of life* itself!" She craned over the book. "Listen to the next verse:

"And Ragnorak will come at last
And end the Norse gods' reign,
And all the leaves of Yggdrasil
Will fall as golden rain."

Emma let out a low whistle. "So according to this, taking the arrowhead did more than just get Odin mad. It set off the beginning of the end! The end of the world. . . *All* the worlds! No wonder Odin has to have it back." Skuli gave an uncomfortable laugh. "But this is all just supposed to be a myth, right? Odin, I mean? And Ragnorak?"

Ragnorak. The end of the world. Jack turned the page. His fingers tightened on the edge of the paper. The pictures of the plagues – they were so like the ones carved on the standing stone. *And the blank panel? The one for the plague of fire?* His fingers scrambled to turn over. *Would this book show the missing picture?*

But the next page was missing. All that was left was a ragged edge.

"Read the next bit of the ballad, Jack," urged Emma. "Go on."

*"So will the arrowhead bring four plagues
And feed men's worst desires
For by plague fire can the gold return
To Asgard's hallowed shire."*

Jack paused. "What are 'men's worst desires', do you think?"

Emma shrugged. "The worst sides of their natures, maybe?"

"Remember how nasty your gran was in the *kafé*?" said Skuli.

"I've never seen her like that before." Jack grimaced. "And Petter didn't seem to care about people being killed either." He read on quickly:

*"But a single other way there is
To set the cursed gold free,
On a death boat under midnight sun
Through the toil of warriors three."*

Jack heard Skuli gasp. "Death boat?"

Seek another way to send the arrowhead back. Those were the words Tor had carved in the ice; what he'd written on Jack's window.

Flames over water. . . Jack's skin prickled. *A midnight sun.* It was all starting to make sense at last. And from Skuli and Emma's expressions, he could tell they were getting it as well.

"There surely be another way
To send the arrowhead home,
Carried by warrior true of heart
On a blazing death boat lone."

Jack gave a short, disbelieving laugh. Sno caught his mood and leapt about, growling and barking.

"The warrior true of heart; I guess that's Tor," said Emma shakily. "But a Viking funeral? By *tonight*?"

"We need a boat," said Jack, nodding. "We need to get Tor inside, holding the arrowhead, and have the whole thing launched on the bay and burning under the midnight sun."

"Nothing too major then," said Emma.

"But we have to do it somehow!" said Skuli.

"Else will all life expire," muttered Jack grimly. He thought about that last blank panel on the standing stone and swallowed. He looked back at the ballad.

"When fire, water, air, earth unite
In the light of a midnight sun,

The curse is broke; the gold is freed
The evil is undone.

Daemon birds, a spell shall weave
To—"

He stopped and looked up the stairs to the front door. There was a tapping sound. Sno padded to the bottom step and growled, low and hostile, from deep inside his throat.

The candlewicks flared, sending shadows leaping up the walls. There was the smell of melting wax and smoke.

There it was again. *Tip-tap. Tip-tap.*

"It could be the kids!" hissed Emma. "Maybe they've worked out where we are!"

The tapping got louder. The door banged against its frame. Then, before they could move, it flew open, knocking over the chest of drawers that held it shut, sweeping the room with a gust of freezing rain. . .

But the doorway was empty. Jack rushed up the stairs to slam it closed. Heart hammering, he peered out at the drenched street, but he couldn't see anyone there. He slid the bolts across, pushed the drawers back in place.

"I thought it was a *beak* tapping," said Emma with a shaky laugh when Jack came back down. "It was just as you were reading that line about the ravens. I've really got the jitters. It was just the rain!"

Just the rain? thought Jack. He picked at his coat and teased something out from the fabric. A feather. A downy, black feather.

He forced his mind back to the ballad. Sno lay at his feet, head resting on his paws, staring up the stairs, ears huge.

"Daemon birds, a spell shall weave
To calm the elders' hate,
And with blood runes will mark the Three
To protect them from their fate.

"That fits what happened in the *kafé*!" Jack broke off. "I saw ravens outside. Remember, Skuli? When the adults started getting really nasty, it was the *ravens* that made them sick. They were at the window, scratching at the glass and stuff!"

Skuli nodded hard. "Imagine if the grown-ups were left to wander round acting as mean as the kids!"

Emma looked confused. "But if the ravens are that helpful, then why don't they make those crazy kids ill as well?"

Jack skimmed ahead. "Maybe here's your answer," he said.

"Elders to fevered sleep shall fall
Through the daemon ravens' power,
But the ravens' power is then made weak
And the Youngers' hate grows fire.

Jack got to his feet and started pacing about. "But it *still* doesn't explain what these ravens are all about and why we're the only sane ones!"

Skuli took the book and read on:

"Three warriors alone remain
When children murderers be,
To break the arrowhead's deadly curse
To set the boat to sea."

"Warriors?" said Emma, shaking her head. "Hang on," said Skuli. "There's a bit more."

"Friend or foe, the daemon birds?
Did they take the Norse boy's life?
Or do they have some higher aim,
A fitting sacrifice?

"No idea what that means," he said, "but that's it. The last page is missing, look."

"So the boat," said Emma impatiently, "what about the boat?"

Jack stopped pacing and looked at them. "Steal one from the harbour?"

"Steal one?" Emma didn't look impressed.

"Well, we could say we're just borrowing it," said Skuli, "but I don't think we're going to be able to give it back – unless the owner doesn't mind floating about on burnt lumps of wood."

Jack laughed and Emma looked at him sternly.

"We could use my dad's boat," said Skuli, uncertainly. "If it was between that and Ragnorak, I think he'd be OK about it."

"So Vikings had funerals in clapped-out fishing boats, did they?" shot back Emma.

Jack and Skuli exchanged uncomfortable glances.

Emma shook her head at them. "I didn't read anything in the ballad about using a boat called *For Cod's Sake* with wonky planks and peeling paint! Haven't really thought this one through, have you?"

"Emma's right, Jack." said Skuli. "It can't be just *any* boat! It has to be a proper Viking boat or it might not get Tor to Valhalla with the arrowhead."

Jack's face went hot. "But where are we going to get a proper Viking boat before midnight tonight?" he said. "It's impossible!" He saw Emma's mouth twitch. A small smile of triumph. "*What?*"

Skuli was grinning too now, like something had just dawned on him.

"Come on, guys!" Jack said. "What's going on?"

"We need a boat like *this one* I made earlier," said Skuli. He took a model boat off a shelf with a flourish and waggled it in front of Jack.

Emma nodded and gave a lopsided smirk. "Bit small for Tor though, don't you think?"

Jack turned the boat in his hands, playing along with the joke, whatever it was. Glee radiated from his friends' faces and it was infectious. "Pretty good work, Skuli," he said. "You're not just an origami master then!"

"Ah, that's just a replica," said Skuli. "The real thing's in the Isdal Museum."

Emma's grin widened. "And that's the boat we're going to steal!"

Excitement prickled Jack's skin. "You're kidding, right? I heard Petter – it's a *priceless national artefact*!"

Emma laughed. "*Course* it is! It's the genuine article!"

Jack stared at them. Skuli's eyes shone.

"It's there and waiting!" said Emma. "Ready for the Festival. Ready to be launched as the midnight sun sets and everything. It happens every year." She gave a twirl. "You said you wanted to steal a boat. Why not do it in style?"

"But Petter won't just let us wheel his prize boat out and burn it to a crisp, will he?" said Jack.

"He'll be in his sickbed by now," said Skuli. "Just like the rest – he won't have any idea what's going on."

"Maybe it's the boat's destiny," said Emma, all serious again, her voice dropped to a whisper. "Ever thought of that? Maybe that was why it was found here; why it waited in the ground all those centuries. Why *now*; right before the night of the midnight sun? Bit of a coincidence, don't you think?"

Jack looked at the model boat in his hands, its elegantly curving hull and its dragon's-head prow. His heart beat faster. *The boat's destiny. Our destiny. . .* As if breaking the law mattered now anyway. He thought of Mum and Gran and Gramps lying ill, the kids loose on the streets. There weren't any more laws.

"We need to get to the museum," he said, and they hurried to the bottom of the steps. "We'll have to find a way to break in and then. . ."

Jack paused, holding his breath, hand raised for the others to stop. It was there again. That tapping sound outside the door. Only this time louder.

Tip-tap. Tip-tap. Not like rain. More like. . .

Before Jack could react, the door crashed open with a blast of icy rain and he lurched back with a cry. The room was filled with whirring wings; slicing claws. Two huge ravens swooped. Emma gasped, covering her head; Skuli swiped his arms desperately. Sno bit at the air in a frenzy.

Demon ravens. Demon ravens.

There was a searing pain on Jack's arm as his skin was slashed. He cried out as black wings dropped towards him again, sharp beaks wide and shrieking. The ravens' talons tore at his flesh and he heard Skuli and Emma scream.

Sno barked wildly, leaping and snapping, then lunged, stretching his body upwards. Jack saw his bared teeth, heard his jaws crunch. . .

The room swirled. Jack's vision went hazy. Grey shadows grew and spread and pressed down on him. . .

Down. . .

Down the spiral steps runs Tor, his face tight with drying blood. Down and down and down. Candles burn in alcoves and grey shadows swing wildly over the curving walls.

A door, studded with black spikes. He rattles the handle, but it is locked. A dead end.

The silence is thick and heavy like earth. Then quick

footsteps echo from above. He listens to them getting louder and stands tensed to fight.

"Find the key."

Tor spins round. The muffled voice on the other side of the door calls out in Norse again. "Above the door plinth, behind the skull stone. Hurry!"

Tor stretches up. Finds the stone; lifts down a key. Feels for the lock and twists the key with both hands.

"Quickly," comes the voice.

Tor heaves the door open. Darts through. Drags it shut as the monk comes into view and lunges with his sword. He swipes at the bolt. Feels the shudder as metal strikes wood. *The key!* he thinks. It is still on the other side of the door, he dropped it in his haste.

From the shadows someone shouts an angry command and the banging on the door stops, and footsteps retreat upwards.

Tor's eyes adjust to the candlelit murk, looking for something to use as a weapon. He peers through the smoke coiling up from incense sticks. Runes are etched into the circular stone walls, and strings of small bones, bird skulls, claws, glossy feathers hang down beside them.

The outline of a figure moves forward. Another monk in a sackcloth robe. His hair clings to his scalp like white cobwebs. Dark eyes stare from his deeply grooved face as he walks, leaning on a stick.

"Tor," he says. There is no harshness in his voice, only compassion and a great sadness. "So it is time," he continues, as if to himself.

"How do you know my name?" Tor says. "How do you

speak my tongue?"

"You are wounded," the old man says. He dips a cloth in a basin of water and gently cleans the blood from Tor's forehead with frail fingers, then rubs an ointment over the wound.

"Why are you helping me?" falters Tor. "I'm not one of you."

"No?" The old monk points at a gold object on the table. "Take it," he says.

This old monk must be mad, thinks Tor. *That's why he is kept locked down here with his bird bones.*

"I choose to be locked here," says the monk, as if reading his thoughts. "I am the gold's keeper. *Take it!*" He watches Tor intently.

Tor hesitates. Candles throw nets of shadows on to the walls. He lifts the arrowhead and gazes at it, at its brilliant sheen, at the delicate patterns curving across its surface; the twisting line fusing so you couldn't see the start and you couldn't see the end. . .

"It is stolen gold," the old man whispers, his voice catching. "Cursed gold."

The arrowhead sits in the hollow of Tor's hand; it fits his palm exactly. And all at once he knows that everything the monk speaks is true.

"The arrowhead has deep and terrible powers," the monk continues. "Men will kill to possess it. It twists their natures. And if not contained it will unleash untold destruction. Plagues of the elements: air, water, earth and fire."

The old monk breaks into a rasping cough, then

moves slowly to touch the stone wall. "This underground sanctuary dulls the arrowhead's force. I am one of a holy order charged to safeguard it."

"But the attack!" cries Tor, tearing his eyes away from the gold, remembering the bodies littering the grass. "The brothers of my clan!"

The old monk lays a hand gently on his shoulder. "Many of *my* brothers are also slain today."

Tor hears a soft clicking caw and shrinks back.

Perched in an alcove, amidst the bones, there are two huge ravens.

The old monk takes a sharp breath. "They have appeared again," he says uneasily.

No earthly bird could be so huge, thinks Tor. "What *are* they?"

"Do you not recognize them?" the old monk says. "They are servants of your god, Odin. Your god of hanged men."

Huginn and Muninn? How can this be? Tor's back presses against cold stone. "Why are they here?" he stammers.

"I do not know their purpose," the old monk says. "The ravens have their own plan perhaps. One that is not Odin's. They have powers too. But the ravens' power is not without limits and . . ." – he stops, stares into their faces as if in some secret communication – ". . . perhaps . . ." – he shuffles closer to Tor, glancing at the birds as if for confirmation, a glimmer of hope in his age-ravaged face – ". . . perhaps *you* will be the one to return the arrowhead."

One of the birds runs a sharp, black beak through its feathers.

"Tor." The monk leans heavily on his stick, his breath

trembling. "You must promise to be the arrowhead's guardian."

Tor shakes his head, tries to hand the arrowhead back, but the monk's look pins him. "You must agree, but freely. A forced promise is no promise."

Ravens and monk are motionless, all three watching him.

Tor's fingers close around the arrowhead. The gold feels strangely warm against his skin, strangely heavy, and as he holds it, whispered words trickle through his mind. *Send the arrowhead back. Flames over water. A midnight sun. . .*

There is the noise of a key in a lock and before Tor can react the door bursts open and a man storms into the room.

"Vekell!" Tor shouts. Instinctively he hides the arrowhead in his sleeve.

The ravens vanish.

Tor sees the old monk hurl a dagger, grazing Vekell's shoulder, but the tall man lurches at him, punching him to the ground, then stands over the monk, an axe raised in his hand.

"Vekell! *Stop!*" Tor holds his brother's arm, trying to wrestle the weapon from him, but is knocked savagely away, crashing against the stone wall, scattering bird bones. He struggles to his feet. "Vekell! *Listen! Stop!*"

Tor sees his brother's axe swing. Blood sprays from the monk's chest as he falls.

Tor scrambles to the monk's side. Blood trickles from the corner of the old man's mouth as he speaks, so quietly that only Tor can hear. "Promise! The plagues will be set in motion!

Ten centuries have passed; this sanctuary is spent. Find another. Bury it deep. Until the right time comes. *Promise!*"

Tor sees the old monk struggle to breathe; under him spreads a dark red pool. "Yes," he whispers. "I promise."

A small smile touches the old monk's lips. Then he strains forward towards Tor's ear, clutching at his arm. "But know this. He who kills me steals not only my life but. . ." There is blood on the old monk's teeth. "A–growing– power–to–control–others." Then his dark eyes glaze and his shattered chest goes still.

Vekell stands over the body. He prods it with the stained edge of the blade and turns it over with his foot. Then he drags Tor up by the throat. "Why did you defy me?" He punches him hard in the ribs and drags him out of the room and up the spiralling staircase. Tor's feet scramble on the stone steps. Up and up and out into the open.

The sky growls with thunder. Flames curl from the flower window of the monastery. "All dead!" Vekell cries with choked sobs as they pass the trail of bodies, monks and Norsemen, and make for the shore. "All our clan brothers dead! What happened? What kind of monks are *these*!"

Tor feels a stab of pity for his brother. "It's not your fault."

But Vekell is not listening. He is rummaging round the bodies of the monks, flinging anything of value into a sack: jewelled beads, a silver chalice. . . Tor clutches at the arrowhead, unpleasantly warm against his skin. But he can feel it slipping from his sleeve. . . And before he can stop it, the gold has fallen to the floor.

Vekell stoops to seize it. "What's this?" He steps back

from Tor to look. The surface glistens, light and dark and darker.

"You thought you would hide it from me, did you?" Vekell slaps Tor full in the face. His eyes widen wildly. "All dead!" he roars, voice cracking, face twisting. The arrowhead is cutting through his hand as he grasps it. Lines of blood drip from his wrists. But he doesn't seem to care. "*All dead!* Our clan will judge me! They will not honour me as chief when Father dies!" He grips Tor's shoulders. "You must not tell what happened here!" The arrowhead reflects light across Vekell's eyes. "*You will not tell!*"

Tor twists free and scrambles away through the dirt, but he is caught and hauled to his feet. Vekell holds the back of Tor's neck and brings the arrowhead close to his mouth.

"No!" Tor punches at Vekell's chest. "Stop!"

Vekell looms over him. "Like secrets, don't you, little brother?" He clamps Tor's jaw in his fist.

There is a deafening crash as part of the monastery roof collapses. Sparks fly up from the ruined timber.

"This will help you to keep secrets!" Vekell grabs Tor's face, squeezes to prise open the teeth.

Tor tries to scream. He feels the blade in his mouth, metal against teeth, warm gold against his tongue.

"You made me do this!" says Vekell, drawing back. "You were the one who turned brother against brother with your deceit!"

Tor's mouth fills with blood. He tries to speak, but cannot. He is dizzy with the pain. His vision goes hazy. Grey shadows grow and spread and press on to him. . .

There is the sound of water crashing onto rocks. . . *Bury it*, a frail voice calls in his mind. *Bury it deep!*

He sees a blur of black smoke spread over the roof of the monastery. Ash is swept like ragged feathers from the walls of the tower on a strange new breeze. Then two birds rise from its turrets. Two dark birds fly out over the crashing water.

14
PROTECTION RUNES

Power against the enemy who travels over the earth.
THE NINE HERBS CHARM

Jack woke up, the visions melting away. *The arrowhead!* He bolted up and scrambled to check his pocket. It was still there; still warm.

"The door was bolted," Skuli muttered. He was propped against the wall, his sleeves hanging in bloody shreds. Emma gave a low moan; the arms of her jacket were also torn to rags.

Jack stared at the mess of overturned chairs, scattered glass and blood. A wreath of smoke spiralled from a dead candle. The rain lashed on the windows and small trickles of water ran down the steps from under the door.

He sat down heavily. Sno rested his head on Jack's knees and he stroked his muzzle. There was something trapped between the dog's teeth. Jack pulled out a ragged black feather. "I think he got one of them," he said with an effort. He remembered the crunching sound, the snap of bone.

Emma eased off her jacket, wincing.

Jack rolled up his sleeves and hobbled to the sink. He put his forearms under the tap, turned it on and drew his breath in sharply as the icy water hit his skin. He flexed his fingers over the red-streaked basin, then splashed water on his face and bent his head to drink some. He looked again at the raw marks, then paused, peering more closely. The cuts were clotting so quickly . . . and they weren't random scratches. . .

"Clean the blood off!" he cried to the others.

They clustered round the basin, flinching as they peeled the ruined fabric from their wounds. Then, huddling close to the candlelight, they stared at their arms.

"They're runes!" gasped Emma. "The same on each of us!"

"The same as the ones in the ice cave," Jack said.

"*Protection runes!*" Skuli cried, eyes wide.

"The ravens must think we need protecting," Jack said quietly.

He took a deep breath, then told them about his vision, about the old monk giving Tor the arrowhead and what he had said about the ravens.

"Hang on!" Skuli scrambled to find the ballad. "*The raven pair. . . And with runes of blood will mark the Three to protect them from their fate.*"

Jack thought suddenly about the power cut. He remembered what Gramps had said about the cables being clawed through. If it hadn't been for that first blackout he never would have been able to follow Tor to the standing stone without being seen.

"And when I was coming out of the ice cave, Skuli," Jack said, when he'd told his friends his theory. "I saw the ravens and that prevented me from stepping on the weak ice! I still fell, but if I hadn't stopped to look at the birds. . ."

"That probably saved you," nodded Skuli.

"The ravens are definitely helping us!" said Jack.

"But *why*?" said Emma.

Skuli took a breath. "Cos we're the Three."

Jack and Emma both let out a laugh of disbelief.

"Think about it," persisted Skuli. "The arrowhead cut us, remember? Me when I first found it. Jack the first time he held it. Then Emma in the fight."

"Yes!" exclaimed Emma. "That's exactly when I started feeling normal again!"

"True," said Jack, frowning. "But the arrowhead cut *Lukas* as well, and he still wants to hang us."

"But it cut us three *first*," said Skuli. "And remember how the marks just disappeared?"

Jack fingered his arm. Something strange was happening to the raven scratches too. Already they were scabbing over, sealing on to the flesh in hard red-purple lines. He watched in fascination as the marks moulded with his skin and became scars.

Skuli picked up the ballad book from the floor and leafed quickly back through the pages. "*Three warriors alone remain*," he read, "*when children murderers be.* We're the Three, whether we like it or not."

"The question is," said Emma, running a hand over the scars on her arm, "how much of a protection are these runes going to be against those kids?"

"Let's find out." Jack jumped to his feet. "Got spare clothes, Skuli? And waterproofs? The darker the better. We need to go to the museum and get the boat on to the water."

"The suspension footbridge," said Skuli, rushing to pull clothes from a wardrobe. "That's the only way to and from the museum."

Jack checked his watch. "We've less than nine hours until midnight. Sno, you're staying here."

"But if the ravens have the power to put adults to sleep," said Emma, grabbing clothes from the pile Skuli had dumped in front of them, "why do they need *us* at all? Why not just carry the arrowhead back to Valhalla themselves?"

"Maybe they can't," said Jack, pushing his head through the neck of a sweater. "Maybe that's not the way Odin wants it done. He's their master. Their power's got limits too, right?" He held up the scrawny feather that had been in Sno's mouth. "That's why they can't make the kids sick." He remembered the old monk's words suddenly. *They have their own plan perhaps. One that is not Odin's.*

"Ready?" said Skuli, from inside the hood of his coat.

The rain swept on to Jack as he opened the door. Back hunched, he stepped out, the others close behind.

The drops lashed down. Low, dark clouds made the afternoon seem like night, draining the colour from the street. Jack slipped round the side of buildings, beckoning the others to follow. Water poured from a broken gutter and small streams swirled round their ankles. Wet seeped into Jack's boots.

"The second plague," Skuli mouthed at him.

Jack felt a tight knot in his chest as they hurried on. Then he drew sharply to a stop. The window of the grocery store was smashed. Kids were darting about inside, stealing things from shelves.

Jack, Skuli and Emma crouched to run past. Then they waited, huddled in a side alley to check the rest of the street was clear. The rain drummed hard on the row of bins beside them, sending bullets of water upwards.

A group of kids appeared, as if from nowhere, coming closer.

In a flash, Jack pulled up his sleeve and signalled for the others to do the same. They raised their forearms. Jack saw the kids hesitate, then change direction.

"The protection runes work!" Emma hissed.

They pressed on through the downpour in the direction of the sea. Jack stayed silent. He had noticed something as he'd shaken down his sleeve. The runes looked less purple-red. As if they were very, very slowly disappearing, and as if using them had made them fade faster.

The last few houses on the western side of town petered out, and Jack heard the thundering river and saw the narrow suspension footbridge that would take them over the gorge. Then it was down to the shore and along the boardwalk to the museum.

As they crossed the footbridge in single file, Jack looked down and saw with a start how the river level was rising. The current had clawed great clods of soil from its banks. The water churned and frothed far below them.

Once off the bridge they went down the steep track to the pebble beach, then followed the wooden boardwalk beside a curved stretch of shoreline. Before long the squat museum building came into view, all stainless steel and concrete.

They sheltered by the glass door of the front entrance. "We'll have to get in somehow," said Jack. "Find a window we can break or. . ." He hesitated, thinking he saw a movement inside, a brief flicker of light. . . But there was nothing. Tentatively he pushed at the glass door and, to his surprise, it swung open.

They edged into the foyer and stood for a few moments, listening. But there was no sound other than the steady metallic rattle of the rain on the roof.

"*Norse longboat.*" Emma pointed at a sign. "This way."

Passing quickly through the room, they saw three wax models of Vikings dressed for battle; a long glass case containing bits of pottery and silver bracelets; and gold coins laid out on red cloth. caught Jack's eye and he hovered to look: a silver goblet and jewelled beads with a crucifix, arranged neatly round an information card. They seemed strangely familiar.

MANY ENGLISH TREASURES WERE
BROUGHT TO SCANDINAVIA
FROM RAIDS ON ENGLISH MONASTERIES.

He leaned close and his breath fogged the glass. *They're the same*, he thought in amazement. The same things he'd seen Vekell steal from the monastery.

"Jack." Skuli nudged him and pointed at the doorway in front of them. "The boat's through there."

Emma gripped Jack's arm. He took a breath and they went in.

15

DRAGON BOAT

There at the harbour stood a ship with
curving prow, eager to depart.

BEOWULF

Jack stared at the boat, his skin prickling.

A huge dragon's head rose over them, its wide mouth filled with runes. Along the curving hull, flowers and pine branches and metal shields caught the light from glass wall at the end of the room. But to Jack the boat seemed to shine with a light of its own. The dark wood of the dragon's neck was carved with swirling serpents, the mouth of one biting the tail of another in a mass of bodies.

"Gripping beasts," Emma. "To scare off evil spirits."

"It's the same boat!" said Jack breathlessly. "The one Tor sailed in for the raid!"

"Are you sure?" said Emma.

"One of the dragon's eyes is damaged," Jack said rapidly. "See? It's got a cross-shaped split in the wood. And the anchor –

look at what it's held by! I remember that snake design, and that metal anchor chain. It's definitely the same boat!"

Standing on tiptoe, he peered between the dragon's teeth at the long snaking tongue and the row of runes carved along it, straining to read them. *"Our glorious chieftain. . ."* he murmured. *"Vekell the Great. Son of Tomas."*

Jack saw that the boat was nestled in a metal cradle; should be easy enough to launch from that – so far so good.

The cradle's wheels sat in rails leading to the glass wall, which looked straight out over the grey water of the inlet; that part would be a bit more tricky. A smudge of light in the grey sky told Jack where the sun was. Rain streamed down the panes, and on the other side Jack saw more rails, sloping down and disappearing into the water. He scanned the glass for some way to get it open. He nodded grimly; he'd it if he had to.

He turned back to the boat. "See the pulleys and ropes?" His eyes narrowed as he worked out the set-up. "Loosen that one there, Skuli," he said, pointing to a rope looped in a figure-of-eight round a bracket on the wall. "Emma – grab this end."

"It's a lot of weight to shift, but I think we can do it," said Skuli.

"It'll need all three of us pulling at once, so wait till I say," Jack replied. He went over to the glass and rattled the handles he found welded into the frame. "Just got to get this open first. . ."

He broke off. He turned to the doorway they'd come in through, frowning, then took a few steps towards it. There was a voice, muffled, echoing along the walls from somewhere in the museum: a man's voice, eerily singsong, reciting some kind of poem.

Jack crept closer to the door, motioning the others to be silent as he listened. Something about the raid on the monastery... Lines about Vekell being some kind of hero, saving Odin's arrowhead from demon monks... The voice got louder. Something about the monks' dead spirits turning into ravens and attacking the boat, killing everyone except Vekell and Tor...

THE SAGA OF VEKELL

A longboat sailed upon the tide,
*   For Odin's gold it yearned.*
But though the crew twelve strong began,
*   Yet only two returned.*

On England's shores did Vekell land,
*   And plundered well and brave,*
And by great Vekell's steadfast hand
*   Was Odin's arrow saved.*

And then for home the longboat sailed,
*   Vekell and brother Tor,*
But it wasn't long, in the dead of night,
*   That the moonlit sky did roar.*

A shout went up from the homebound deck
*   As terrible clouds drew near,*
Demons of the slain whirred down

And the winds of fate did veer.

In raven form the demons came,
Beaks stabbed down as rain,
And despite the valour of their lord,
All men, save Tor, were slain.

Brave Vekell fought the traitor Tor
Upon the icy waste,
To free all Isdal from the plagues
And the dreadful doom they faced.

With wit and stealth did Vekell fight,
With swordship skilled and fast,
And Tor did fall to his icy doom,
And the traitor thus was smashed.

And noble Vekell pledged that day
A heavy sacrifice,
For Odin's gold lay out of reach,
Lost deep in tomb of ice.

And though his earthly life will pass,
Great Vekell waits alone,
Ready to return again,
To carry the arrowhead home.

"He's getting closer!" Jack pulled at Skuli and Emma's sleeves. There were footsteps, heading steadily in their direction.

"Hide! Over there!"

The three of them rushed to the other end of the room and huddled in the murk behind a display board, peering through the gap where the hinges attached the panels together.

Jack saw the silhouette of a figure moving by the boat. The male voice continued to speak, distorted by echoes.

"Unearthed on this very spot. . ."

Jack's pulse raced. Why was he talking to himself? Why wasn't he in bed with the fever like the other adults?

". . .Vekell declared that on his death he should be buried in the same ship in which he took that fateful journey. . ."

Vekell? Jack held his breath as the man passed right by them.

". . .until that day when the arrowhead is found once more. . ."

Jack's eyes strained to adjust to the gloom. The man stood with his back to them, stooped over some kind of long glass box raised up from the floor. A match flared and a candle flame rose inside a metal lantern, spreading a ghostly glow over the case. There were bones inside, a skeleton laid out in an open glass coffin. And as the glass lit up, Jack saw a face reflected in it, merged with the gnarled human skull inside.

Petter!

"Still not at rest," Petter sighed. He took out a heavy bunch of keys, slipped one into the lock and lifted the lid, the keys left hanging.

Candlelight spread up the wall behind the case and Petter reached to unhook the clothes hanging there – a tunic edged with pale snakes, a mangy fur cloak. A Viking helmet with a faint design of wolves.

Jack stared, the rune scars on his arms prickling. The colours were dull with age, but he recognized those things!

Petter leant over the coffin, laying Vekell's clothes gently inside, tucking them round the bones. He was breathing fast. Sweat trickled down his face and his normally neat hair was dishevelled. There was a dark stain under each armpit and his eyes seem to bulge behind the thick lenses of his glasses.

Jack's arms stung. There was a frenzy of rain on the roof over them, like beaks tapping.

Petter stretched up, unclipped an axe from the wall and brought it down, sagging under its weight at first. Then his whole body trembled, and suddenly he was lifting it easily with one hand. Then he ran one palm slowly and deliberately over the blade.

Jack winced, watching the blood trickle down Petter's fingers and drip off their tips. Fat red splashes dropped on to the bones below. He remembered Vekell attacking the old monk – with that same axe? The old man's words to Tor as he was dying. *He who kills me steals not only my life but a growing power to control others.*

Realization hit. That voice Jack had heard Petter speak with in the *kafé*! the man with the scarred lips in his visions. . .

Vekell! Jack shuddered and the floorboard under him let out a high-pitched creak.

Petter brought his head up sharply and spun round. "Who's there?"

Jack held his breath. He felt Emma and Skuli tense beside him.

"I know you're there! *Come out!*"

Jack saw the whites of Emma's eyes as she held on to his arm and he rapidly shook his head. He tried to breathe evenly. "Only use runes if you have to," he mouthed. "Door. When I say."

Petter tore back the screen and stood there looking at them, the axe rested on the floor. He threw down his glasses and narrowed his eyes.

"The entrance door was open," said Jack slowly. "We're doing a school project and. . . Anyway, we're going now."

Petter continued to stare.

"You really have some wonderful artefacts, Petter," said Emma.

Jack heard her struggle to keep the fear out of her voice. *Keep talking,* he thought. *Find a way to escape.*

"We saw the amazing Viking jewellery on the way in," he said steadily, turning his head a little in Emma and Skuli's direction, flicking his eyes towards the doorway, shifting one foot ever so slightly towards it.

"My mum made jewellery," said Skuli randomly, talking too fast. "We've kept all her tools."

Petter stepped closer, edging them towards the boat. Out of the corner of his eye, Jack saw Skuli ease the bunch of keys from the glass case and slip it in his pocket.

Jack felt the arrowhead, warm against his skin. Petter was by the narrow doorway now, blocking their only way out, one fist still clutching the axe handle. He stared at his reflection in the rain-streaked glass wall and the grey water beyond.

Then Jack blinked hard. Instead of a reflection of Petter, he saw another man reflected there, much taller, broader. . .

And as Petter turned, it was no longer the museum curator Jack saw.

Skuli gave a stifled cry and the three scrambled back in a huddle.

Emerald snakes coiled over the hem of the man's tunic, his thick muscle filling the fabric. His fur cloak was streaked with rich earth colours, and wolves leapt in bright silver across his helmet. Blonde plaits hung down, tied with strings of sharp teeth.

In front of them stood Vekell himself.

"But *how*. . .?" Emma gasped.

Vekell lifted the axe, as if the weight of it were nothing. "Tor." His scarred mouth twisted into a sneer. "I might have known you would have it."

Petter's gone, Jack told himself, fighting panic. No point trying to understand how it happened. *This is Vekell now. He thinks I'm Tor. He knows I have the arrowhead. Play along.*

He moved around the boat, trying to draw Vekell away from Skuli and Emma. He forced his voice into fake confidence. "I've kept it from you all these years."

Axe resting on his shoulder, the man stepped towards Jack. "Give it to me."

Jack edged away. His shoulders pressed against the hull of the boat and he reached back, scrabbling about with his fingers, grasping only a useless fistful of papery petals. He felt a cramp of fear but he continued to hold Vekell's gaze. "We both lost brothers that day."

Vekell's voice was low, dangerous. "Give me the arrowhead."

"I don't think you understand." Jack's shaky fingers closed round a pine branch, spiky with needles. He glimpsed Skuli and Emma slowly moving in on each side of Vekell. "If anyone takes the arrowhead back to Odin. . ." he gripped the sharp branch in his fist – ". . .*I* will!"

With a shout he flung the branch hard into Vekell's face. The man gave a bellow and Jack sprang away as the axe swiped the air. Shouting, Emma kicked hard at Vekell's legs. There was a blur of movement as Skuli charged forward, and Vekell lost his balance and crashed down.

"Quick," hissed Jack. "Now! *Run!*"

They tore down the corridor to the main entrance and Jack rattled the handle.

"It's *locked*?" gasped Emma.

"The keys, Skuli!" Jack cried. "You have Petter's keys, right?" Skuli pulled them out and started trying them in the lock, fumbling to find the right one.

Jack heard noises from the boat gallery; running footsteps getting closer.

"*Come on*!" Skuli said through gritted teeth as he tried another key.

Jack glanced over his shoulder. Vekell appeared at the end of the corridor, axe swinging by his side. With a shout he charged straight at Jack.

Jack moved away from the others and stood his ground, his hands in fists at his side. Heart hammering, he saw the axe come at him, saw the razor edge of it glint as he hurtled closer. *Closer. Closer. . .*

At the very last moment, Jack threw himself to one side. The axe swung down and bit into the wood floor with a sickening thud. He scrambled away on all fours and jumped back on to his feet as Vekell tugged the handle to free it.

"The protection runes!" Jack shouted "Now!" Emma came close, yanking up the sleeves of her coat.

"I *will* have the arrowhead!" Vekell wrenched the axe from the floor and made a savage swipe. Jack felt the force of it sweep past. He twisted to avoid it, the side of his face smacking against the glass of the door. He hauled himself to his feet, light exploding through his head, and copied Emma, lifting his arms, runes exposed. He saw Vekell hesitate, but then tighten his grip on the shaft of the axe and lurch forward.

"You too, Skuli!" Emma screamed. "The Three together!"

Skuli tugged at his sleeves. The axe was in the air again as the three of them stood, shoulder to shoulder, their arms raised high.

Vekell stopped, swaying a little. His face twisted and his eyes blazed, but he came no nearer. The axe slipped from his hand and Jack shot out a foot to kick it away.

It gave Skuli the time he needed. He leapt back to the lock. There was the clatter of metal, the click of a key turning, and they rammed the door open, tumbling forward and out into a shock of cold air and driving rain.

And they ran.

16

BEWARE, MY BROTHER

Power against three and against thirty.
THE NINE HERBS CHARM

Jack's legs moved mechanically over the pebble shore. His breathing came out in clipped gasps. He couldn't feel pain or cold, just the relentless need to run. Skuli and Emma sprinted ahead of him, kicking up water from the flooded boardwalk.

Jack twisted his head to look behind at the squat grey shape of the museum. The rain drove into his face. Was Vekell following? Emma stumbled and Jack put on a burst of speed to grab her arm and steady her.

The shoreline flashed past. Across the bay a blur of waterfalls spread like white webs over the rock slopes. They sprinted up the steep track towards the gorge. He looked back over his shoulder again but now all he could see was a smothering mass of mist.

How were they going to get Tor to the boat now? he asked himself.

They got to the footbridge. Jack glanced down, past the handrail to the river churning under them, crumbling its earth banks. The water flashed past at a ferocious speed, carrying with it a plank, a car tyre, the corpse of a cat.

Skuli had stopped and was doubled over coughing. His fringe was plastered to his forehead and water dripped down his pale face.

"Come on, Skuli!" Jack's hands trembled as he reached for his arm. "We have to get Tor." He was hit by a pain along his legs and a shock of nausea. He felt the shuddering roar of the river through the soles of his feet. Why did Vekell want the arrowhead so badly that he'd wait all these years for it?

They ran on, up the track on to the deserted main street, water swirling round their ankles. *Past Skuli's house*, Jack recited to himself between short, stabbing breaths, trying to keep calm. *Past the* kafé. *Past the square. Get up Church Lane.*

They reached the *kafé* and through the window Jack saw paper chains ripped and dangling, the telly screen smashed, chairs and tables overturned. He desperately wanted to check on his mum, and Gran and Gramps. He thought of them lying ill in the house next door. And what about Sno, locked in at Skuli's? *There's no time,* he told himself. *Keep moving! Get Tor!*

"Kids!" cried Skuli.

Jack pushed Skuli and Emma into a doorway and

cautiously they peered out. Figures materialized out of the gloom.

"They're everywhere," said Emma. "Look."

Jack craned forward. "Wait. Only move when I say."

They stayed where they were, semi-crouched, but the kids showed no signs of leaving. "I was thinking," whispered Jack, eyeing their movements. "The boat won't light easily, especially if the wood's wet. We'll need something to get it started."

"We go for the sail," said Emma. "It's thin and should catch fast."

"We need to be sure though. Have a backup."

"My dad has a big box of firelighters in our garage," said Emma. She jabbed a thumb. "Five minutes back that way."

Jack frowned. "There's no time for us all to go."

"I'll go on my own," said Emma. "While you two get Tor. It makes sense."

"You're right about lighting the wood," Skuli said anxiously. "But we should stay together."

Jack wiped the rain from his eyes. He didn't like them splitting up either. "But it is quicker that way." He squinted down the street. "OK, Emma, we'll meet at the graveyard. By the church door."

"I'll go straight there." She tightened her hood round her face. "And if I'm late for whatever reason, just go ahead to the museum. I'll catch up."

"Be fast," Jack hissed, his jaw tight, and he watched her dart off into the rain.

Jack nodded at Skuli. "Let's keep moving."

They went on, slipping forward from doorway to doorway, but as they neared the square there were voices, excited chatter.

Jack gestured to Skuli to stay back. He edged round the wall and held his breath. Only metres away, sitting on the lowest branch of the big pine tree, sheltered from the downpour, was Lukas, and a smaller boy in a bright red plastic coat.

Lukas gulped some beer from a bottle, then wiped his mouth with his sleeve. He slipped a cigarette from a half-empty box and lit it.

"If your dad finds out, Lukas!" said the smaller boy with glee.

Lukas sucked on the cigarette and coughed. He grabbed the boy's ear and twisted it hard so he squealed. "Going to tell, are you? Because if you do, I'll string you up!"

He shoved the boy away and threw the cigarette stub on the floor. It sizzled in a puddle. "But guess who's the *first* person I'm going to string up."

"*I* know! *I* know!" the small boy chanted.

Lukas laughed and took another swig of beer. He jumped down from the tree.

More kids appeared from the edges of the square, a lot of them dressed in rain jackets with plastic hats pulled low over their faces. Some of them were dressed up in Festival clothes: the boys in knee-length tunics and helmets, the girls in long dresses that stuck, sodden, to their legs. They congregated round the tree, shouting and laughing.

"We need to get past them," whispered Jack into Skuli's

ear. They quickly moved into the next doorway. They were about to do the same again when a car with blazing headlights came hurtling along the street and they had to crouch low as the beam swept past them like a searchlight. As the light went by, they sprinted forward and hid behind some bins.

Jack peered out. The car skidded to a stop, beeping its horn, and he saw an older kid smirking at the wheel. The kids clustered round it. They clambered on to the bonnet and the roof with whoops of delight, ripping off the wipers, thumping the metal with their fists.

Jack and Skuli crept past, keeping to the shadows.

The car set off again. Jack winced as several kids were thrown off into the road. They hobbled up, grinning. The car accelerated, water spraying up from the wheel rims, then did a tight swerve, bashing into the side of a house so that a pair of stag antlers crashed to the ground, before reversing noisily and speeding into a wild circle.

Kids dashed out of the way, shrieking, then closed back in for more.

Another car joined the game. Then another. The tyres spun, the engines revved. One car hit a lamppost and a hubcap spun off like a deadly frisbee. The kids were screeching with delight, chanting those same words Jack had heard before:

"*Odin's vengeance! Odin's vengeance!*"

"They're mad," said Skuli.

Round and round the square the cars raced, circling the big pine tree in its centre. And then Jack saw it.

Swinging from a branch, the loop of thick rope in a noose.

A car seemed to come at them from nowhere, revving blindly along the road with its mangled wipers. Jack and Skuli sprang to one side and it ploughed on, accelerating, smacking a bin on to its side. In the headlights Jack saw the little boy in the red raincoat, sloshing excitedly in the puddles in the middle of the street.

He'll be hit!

Jack's mind kicked into automatic. His legs swept up sprays of water as he broke into a sprint. "Get out of the way!" he screamed, but the beeping horns and revving engines drowned out his voice. He sprang forward, diving sideways, knocking the boy off his feet and into the water.

Skuli splashed down beside him and together they dragged the boy off the road as the car did a wide arc, ready to swing round again.

The boy's eyelids sprang open, making the two of them start back in surprise. "You're Jack," he hissed as he pulled himself up and staggered away, shouting back over his shoulder, "We're going to hang you."

Jack and Skuli crouched in a doorway, watching as he ran up the road.

"They can't really be planning that, can they, Jack?" said Skuli, his voice gone up a pitch.

"We need to get Tor," Jack muttered, thinking fast. It would only be a matter of seconds before the boy raised the alarm. The kids were driving – why shouldn't *they*? He'd driven his dad's farm truck back home. It'd be way faster than carrying Tor all the way to the museum. "Gran's van," he shouted over the water thundering from overflowing gutters. The van was never locked and Gran kept the key in the glove compartment. "It's parked down at the harbour."

They broke cover and reached the harbour steps, Jack leaping down them three at a time, Skuli close behind. But at the bottom, they stopped short. The quayside was totally flooded, the pier half submerged. Boats jostled like nervous animals in a pen. Jagged waves rose up and smashed down on the shore, loosening and lifting away clods of soil and stones. Grasping fingers of water pulled away the bigger rocks, then came clawing back for more.

Surrounding the harbour Jack saw dozens of gushing waterfalls as huge amounts of water spilled down the mountain slopes into the bay. Along the shore the row of wooden houses creaked as water rose and fell against them.

They got to Gran's van. Water lapped the tyres as they pulled open the doors. But Jack paused before getting in. At the far side of the bay something had caught his eye. A movement of rocks, tumbling down the slick wet mountainside, loosening more rocks on the way. A section of cliff was shifting, sliding. . .

A crack detonated through the air and, as he watched, a whole piece of mountain came right away, hurtling vertically and crashing into the water.

"Get in the van, Skuli," Jack heard himself say, but neither of them seemed able to move, only stare out across the bay, pinned rigid by the sight. In a flash, Jack remembered the carvings from the standing stone. . . He knew what was coming next, but still he couldn't move. He saw the water draw away from the shore as if the tide had gone out suddenly. Rocks were exposed like jagged teeth and boats fell on their sides in the dark mud. Jack heard a hissing sound, like a long, rasping breath, then across the bay he saw a wave rise, like a flap of skin on a gulping grey throat.

A shout went out from behind them and Jack turned to see kids at the top of the steps. The little kid in the red raincoat was with them. Some pointed in their direction; some started running towards them. A car swung down the looping road leading to the harbour, then another. A chant went up. "*Jack! Jack! Jack! Jack!*"

"Get in, Skuli!" Jack flung himself into the driver's seat and slammed the door shut. He found the keys and rammed them into the ignition. The engine growled into life and he shoved it into gear and pressed the accelerator. The steps were a mass of kids. The van shot forward, accelerating with a horrible juddering up the harbour road.

"*Move!*" he yelled at the kids as he looked in his rearview mirror at the white line of water – the wave, the tsunami – sweeping towards the shore, and them.

17

PLAGUE OF WATER

And the Youngers' hate grows fire.
THE ANCIENT BALLAD OF ISDAL

Jack spun the steering wheel and pressed the accelerator, and the van shot forward. Out of the window he saw the wave coming across the bay, a growing line of white.

"*Faster!*" Skuli shouted, his knuckles gripping the dashboard.

The van climbed, straining round the first bend of the looping road. Further up Jack saw kids' cars winding their way towards them and slapped his seatbelt into place with one hand. "Hold on!" He forced the van into gear and put his foot down. He heard the engine roar, the vehicle shudder under him.

At the next bend Jack saw the wave sweep closer, a slick grey mass threaded with white, lifting boats vertically and smacking them down as if they were toys. His back tensed against the driver' seat.

Skuli gave a shout as a car sped towards them, head-on. Jack held the steering wheel tight, keeping the van straight as the car careered at them. "*Come on,*" he muttered. "*Come on.*"

At the last second he swerved violently to one side and the kids' car rocketed past. Skuli was flung against him. Jack righted the wheel. In his rear-view mirror he saw a blaze of red lights as the kids' car slammed on its brakes and clumsily reversed.

More cars sped down the road. Jack twisted the wheel one way and then the other, weaving round them. He winced as a side mirror smashed off. A bonnet clipped the side of the van, knocking it into a spin.

Jack braked, his seatbelt tight across his chest, but the van skidded on towards the road's sheer edge. There was the sound of loose stones churning under the tyres as he struggled to keep control. Skuli yelped. The swaying van came to the very edge of the drop, and ground to a shuddering stop.

Out of the windscreen Jack saw the wave hit. It smacked into a house, knocking it straight into the bay. The houses round it collapsed, wood walls breaking apart and debris swept forward as the water surged on. Channelled by the narrow harbour valley, the water got faster, rising along the road like stretched grey skin.

"Look at that!" Jack yelled as the car furthest down the slope was peeled off the road and carried away, floating and rotating on the heaving water. The other cars were turning hastily, revving back up the road as the water came gushing round them.

Skuli grabbed hold of the handrail. "How high will it come?"

Jack's mind raced. *Mum, Gran, Gramps, Sno. . . Not much further, surely, surely?* He wrenched the van back into gear, reversed off the cliff edge, and strained up the road. He saw water crash up the stone steps, kids racing to get higher. Sea spray thudded the back window. The steering wheel was slippery with sweat. From behind them, headlight beams reflected in the mirror, dazzling him. A car had escaped the water and was following.

Jack got to the top of the slope and accelerated. He made several sharp turns, doubling back then swerving down a narrow track. He slotted the van between two buildings and killed the lights and engine. Moments later, the kids' car roared past.

They sat there a while, Skuli resting his head on the door, Jack slumped back in his seat. Slowly, Jack wound down his window, listening to the eerie quiet.

"You did well," Skuli said at last. He stared ahead, not moving, face pale, and Jack guessed what he was thinking about: the people in those houses; the kids in those cars caught in the wave.

All Jack could manage was, "Carry on?"

He reversed back on to the road and the van crawled forward, the two of them scanning in every direction.

The dark shape of the church loomed against the sky and Jack turned up the lane towards the graveyard, gravel hitting the windscreen.

Skuli fiddled with the radio, catching a few snatches: *Emergency . . . all areas . . . evacuation. . .*

"Turn it up!" said Jack, but the words gave way to a piercing wail of static.

At the top of the road, Jack parked the van and turned off the engine, pushing open the door. The muddy ground gave way a little under his shaky legs.

"Can you see Emma?"

Skuli frowned. "She should be here by now!"

The air was still strangely calm. All Jack could hear was the murmur of the sea in the distance. There were no clouds. The sky was pale blue in every direction and he could see the sun, a dull gold ball, making its long, shallow arc to the horizon. He checked his watch. Only five hours until midnight. From where they stood he could see right down over the town, to the pine tree in the square and beyond to the devastated bay. The sun's yellow light made the rooftops glow like embers.

"The museum will have got the brunt," said Skuli by his shoulder. "What if the longboat got damaged?"

Jack didn't answer. He didn't want to think about that. He looked at the water in the harbour, swirling and sinking, slowly settling back into place. He bit at his nails. How long did they have before the plague of earth kicked in?

He hurried to the back of the van and swung open both doors. "Let's get Tor."

They reached the standing stone and hastily pulled off the branches hiding the body. Jack stared a moment at the face, so like his own. He checked the straps on the stretcher. *Soon, Tor*, he thought, *it'll all be over. . . One way or another.* "Ready to lift? One, two, *three*. . ."

As they carried Tor to the van, Jack remembered the runes carved in the dragon's mouth. *Vekell. . . Son of Tomas.* "Tor. . . Son of Tomas," he said aloud.

"What?" Skuli paused as they eased the stretcher into the back of the van.

Son of Tomas. . . Son of Tomas. . . "Tomassen!"

"Jack Tomassen," said Skuli, nodding. He smiled a little. "Tor really is your long-lost relative, eh?"

They shut the doors and looked around again for Emma. She should come running up the lane any minute. . . Jack walked slowly through the graveyard and back. Still no sign.

"She said not to wait," said Skuli doubtfully. "She said she'd catch us up at the museum."

Jack looked at his watch again. "Let's get back in the car. Maybe we'll meet her on the way back. Keep a lookout."

He started the engine and swung back on to the lane, easing the van down the slope. But no Emma. All the way to the river, they saw no one.

They reached the suspension footbridge, got out and stood on the edge of the gorge, the churning river below them. A car floated past, then a log; then a man's body, too fast to make out the face. Jack stared after it.

Hopefully Vekell has been swept away, he told himself as they unloaded Tor and carried him across the bridge. The handles of the stretcher dug into his palms and the planks under his feet wobbled. He thought about Petter. Was it right to hope that?

They cast long shadows as they made their way along the boardwalk following the edge of the still-high, swirling tide. The sun was noticeably closer to the horizon now. They slowed as they approached the steel and concrete of the museum building, glancing round for any sign of Vekell.

"The water must have blasted through here," said Jack as they reached the shattered glass door. He nodded towards a pile of mangled wood and seaweed. "Let's leave Tor behind there while we check inside."

Heart thumping he went in, Skuli close behind.

They made their way towards the boat, picking their way over a mess of glass and plastic and metal; a broken display case, with gold coins and bits of jewellery scattered about inside; a trio of slumped mannequins dressed in Viking clothes.

They got to the gallery and Jack went first, feeling cold water seep into his boots. Then a wave of relief. "The boat's OK, Skuli!" he said.

Skuli gave a short laugh. "The glass in here must be reinforced."

Jack looked towards the end of the room. The metal windowframes were twisted, the panes covered in cracks, the lower ones still dripping. But the glass wall had held!

Jack smiled back at Skuli. Then he saw his friend's grin fade.

"That's Emma's!" Skuli stooped to lift an archery bow from the wet floor. "I've seen her use it at competitions!" He pointed at the engraved gold plaque on the shaft. "See? Her name's on it."

"And it looks like she tried to use it." Jack pulled out an arrow embedded in the wall. With rising dread he waded round the room, picking up the scattered arrows that floated on the water. Most were broken, their shafts snapped. He found the quiver, and pushed the only intact ones inside. He counted five.

As he stood up he saw something half hidden in an alcove in the wall.

"Her backpack," he said, opening it up. "Firelighters inside, look, and a couple of lighters. Even some kind of blowtorch. She thought of everything."

"She must have decided to come straight here," said Skuli worriedly. "Why, do you think?"

"There must have been a reason or. . ." Jack stopped. He heard a noise close by, back the way they'd come; a patter, like footsteps, then a splashing. He turned round just as a shape appeared at the doorway.

"Sno!" Jack rushed forward and crouched to wrap his arms round the dog's neck. "How did you get out of Skuli's?"

Sno whined. He was limping and his tongue lolled out from his mouth at a funny angle. Jack stroked his fur, finding stiff patches of dried blood. And as he ran his fingers round Sno's collar, he saw that there was something scrawled on it.

Quickly Jack flattened the fur round Sno's neck. He read the words, then reread them. Breathlessly, he unbuckled the collar and pulled it taut.

"*The church,*" he read. "*Only Tor.*
Bring the arrowhead.
Or she dies."

18

RANSOM

To them was naught, the want of gold.
VÖLU SPÂ - THE VALA'S PROPECY

Jack stared at the message and at the handwriting. It was the same looping scrawl he'd seen written on a *kafé* napkin. His fingers tightened on the leather collar. "It's Petter's writing."

"At least that means Emma's still alive," said Skuli. "Doesn't it?"

"Yes," said Jack. "Of course." But he couldn't look Skuli in the eye. He stroked Sno, feeling queasy.

"But why does Petter – Vekell – why does he want the arrowhead so badly?" Skuli gabbled. "And why take Emma back to the church?"

"Maybe he wants to keep the three of us apart," said Jack. "The message says only Tor should go. Me."

Skuli nodded. His voice was tense. "He knows our

protection runes are too strong otherwise. But what about Tor's funeral? What are we going to do?"

Jack wiped his face with the back of his hand, then stood up. "Help me get Tor to the boat."

"And Emma?" said Skuli, rushing after him as he strode back to the entrance and out of the building.

"Do you really think Vekell's going to hand Emma over without being given the arrowhead?"

"But we can't just leave her!"

They lifted the stretcher and carried Tor into the building, stepping over the debris.

You have to send the arrowhead back, a voice in Jack's head told him. *The power's growing. Can't you feel it? Each plague's worse than the last. Look how low the sun is!*

Through the fractured glass, fragments of gold light glinted, and all around him, Jack felt something pressing down. It was hard to describe; like a charge in the air, something gathering and growing.

With a grunt he and Skuli lifted the stretcher up and over the edge of the hull.

Jack looked at Tor, lying in the bottom of the boat. This should have been a special moment, with all three of them to see it. Tor in place after all these centuries, ready for his funeral. Ready to take the arrowhead back.

Jack lay Emma's bow and quiver of arrows by the body. It seemed right, somehow. He put the blowtorch and lighters in there as well, and arranged the firelighters along the hull; waxy bundles of resin-soaked kindling. Then he uncoiled the rope from its bracket on the wall.

"We keep to the plan then, do we?" said Skuli flatly. "Sacrifice one to save all, is it?"

Jack didn't answer. *You've what you need*, the voice inside him soothed. *The arrowhead, Tor, the boat, even the firelighters and blowtorch. Everything's in place. You and Skuli can launch the boat. The plagues are happening all over the world. Emma's just one person.*

Jack slipped his hand into his pocket and his fingers curled protectively around the arrowhead. The gold was pleasantly warm. . .

But she's Emma.

Jack's mind jolted. His hand recoiled. Out of the corner of his eye he glimpsed black wings sweep past the broken windows.

Friend or foe the demon birds?

His throat was tight as he spoke. "We go back to the church," he said. "We go for Emma."

Skuli looked at him, wide-eyed. "Yes, but—"

An idea was forming in Jack's head. Jack took the small blowtorch back out of the hull. "Your mum, Skuli – she made jewellery, right? So you know about that stuff?"

"Yes, I used to watch her when I was younger, but. . ."

"So you'd know how to use this on metal?"

Before Skuli could answer, Jack pulled him back towards the entrance and fished the gold coins from the smashed glass cabinet and floor. He handed Skuli the pieces, then the arrowhead itself.

Skuli nodded as he caught on. "If we melt the surface

of these coins with the blowtorch, we might be able to fuse them, then make an impression. . . But won't our arrowhead melt too?"

"I wouldn't be worried about that!" said Jack. "It's nothing like ordinary gold – you've seen how it can cut through anything! Think you can do it?" he urged. "Make a fake? And fast enough?"

Skuli rotated the coins between his fingers. He nodded. "Yes, maybe."

"Come on then!"

Skuli found a metal surface to work on, then hunted around for other metal scraps to use as tools. He laid out the gold coins and lit the blowtorch, directing the short jet of fire at them. The metal surfaces melted and glowed. Skuli eased them together and Jack watched as, slowly, slowly, he shaped them, finally pressing the arrowhead on top so it hissed and smoked.

The blowtorch flicked off and Skuli wiped the sweat from his top lip. "Just made it before the gas ran out."

Sno brushed up beside Jack, his fur pricking. His body was rigid, and his ears pointed stiffly. Then he let out a low, strange whine.

A shudder ran through the floor. Jack instinctively reached for the wall but almost as soon as it came, the trembling was gone. He stared at Skuli.

Skuli's face was pale. "Some kind of tremor."

The plague of earth, thought Jack, but he kept his thoughts to himself.

He watched Skuli lift the fake arrowhead between two

strips of metal and dip it in a puddle of water on the floor. Coils of steam rose off it.

"It's good, Skuli," said Jack, turning the fake arrowhead over in his hands. "Really good." He held the real arrowhead in his other hand. The weight, the look, everything was virtually the same. Only the engravings were all reversed. Would it fool Vekell? What would he do if he realized? Jack gave Skuli the real one and shoved the fake in his pocket.

Jack wrestled a hooded tunic from an overturned mannequin and tossed it to Skuli. "If we meet any kids, we need to try and blend in." He took another tunic and pulled the soggy material over his head. "Grab that helmet. We'll take clothes for Emma too. Now let's get to the church."

It was only as they headed for the door that the next quake hit, throwing Jack off his feet and against the wall.

There was a crash and a twisting, and a growling lurch . . . then nothing but a hollow, suffocating silence.

Trust not . . .
A croaking raven . . .
A tree with roots broken . . .
Ice new formed . . .
A brother's slayer.

THE HÁVAMÁL

PART 3
EARTH
AND FIRE

Tor. Running on ice, gripping the arrowhead. A growling tremor throws him to the ground, opening cracks around him. He pulls himself up and runs on with a sob. He knows what he must do. There is only one choice left.

"Tor!" A voice roars from behind him. He looks back, sees Vekell gaining, the cold glint of a sword in his hand.

Another tremor hits, sweeping snow from ridges, filling the air with flakes, like a blizzard. The plague of earth, just as the old monk told him. Already air and water have ripped through the village. He stumbles as he thinks of those already dead. The killings.

Tor comes to a stop. It is a dead end. An ice cliff plunges away below him.

He turns and draws his sword, facing Vekell. The wind lifts a sheet of snow off the edge of the ice crest. Strange clouds are gathered round the peak of the Brennbjerg mountain.

"Give me the arrowhead," growls Vekell. His scarred lips are a livid blue. Frost settles in his plaited beard as he comes closer.

This way, the raven whispers to Tor. *It will be safe this way.*

Tor pushes the arrowhead into the deep pocket of his cloak and moves a few steps along the ridge. He turns and draws his own sword. A silent mass of snowflakes twists between him and his brother.

Vekell slashes with his sword, and Tor lunges fast to block it. Sparks flicker where their blades clash. Ice is thrown up under their scuffling feet.

Tor staggers back. Under one heel he feels a movement. The ice slumps and a crack widens under him.

Another quake. The ice beneath Tor gives and his sword spins away. His fingers claw for a grip. His two hands hook on to the thinnest of ledges. His legs kick the void of a crevasse.

Vekell crouches above him, holding out his arm. "I will help you, brother. Reach up to me." But Tor sees that Vekell's eyes are on his cloak, searching greedily for its hidden pocket. The words of the old monk tumble round his head. *Bury it deep. . . Until the right time comes.*

He knows what he must do.

Tor lets go with one hand, but instead of reaching up to Vekell, he lets the arm hang limp by his side. Vekell's eyes widen. "No!" he shouts, straining to reach for him. "I will carry the arrowhead back! You will not take it from me!"

But already Tor's stretched arm is shuddering as, one by one, his fingers start to lose their grip.

It will be safe this way, the ravens soothe. *We will ease your fall.*

Father, Tor whispers in his head. Mother.

And he lets go.

19

THE GOD OF HANGED MEN

No knowledge can save you,
And no magic will save you.
THE DOOM OF ODIN

Jack felt his legs curled under him, cramped and numb. He thought of Tor . . . falling, sacrificing himself to stop the plagues . . . carving runes in the ice cave while he died . . . waiting centuries to be brought to the Viking boat. He thought of the sun getting lower on the horizon. Emma. His family. The people already dead. His head throbbed under his helmet, making him grimace. He pulled himself up, the room coming back into focus. "Skuli? Sno?"

He heard a bark, then there was warm, ragged breath on his face. He rested his head against the thick white fur of Sno's neck for a moment, then heaved himself to his feet.

"Skuli?" Jack saw a movement and stumbled over to help. "Are you OK?"

Skuli wiped the blood off his forehead below his helmet

and blinked hard. "Think so."

"Let's get to Emma then. Grab those Viking clothes for her."

Why did he get the feeling that quake was just for starters?

They left the museum and went quickly back over the footbridge, jumping new gaps where the tremor had ripped planks from the walkway, revealing the dark river far below. Out to sea, Jack saw the yellow sun edged with a deepening orange. The faded blue sky was oddly empty; not even a seagull flew across it. But he saw a strange bank of cloud collected round the Brennbjerg mountain. It swirled up from the peak and oozed down the craggy rock slopes before melting away.

"Forget the van," he said as they reached the other side of the footbridge. "The kids will recognize it."

They reached the town, picking their way over broken roof tiles and cracks in the pavements, tensed for the next tremor. Now and again windows rattled and jagged pieces of glass fell and smashed.

"They're getting stronger," said Skuli, and Jack thought about his mum and Gran and Gramps, ill in bed. They had no way to get out if a bigger quake hit.

Then he saw a movement and gripped Sno's collar, pulling him down. They crouched behind a low wall, watching.

Two cars were burning in the main street. Kids dressed in Viking costumes appeared from doorways. Some with cuts and bruises. A few limped as they ran. They didn't seem bothered by their injuries. They were caught up in something else.

Odin's vengeance. Odin's vengeance. . . Jack heard their shouts, the same words repeated. *Hunt . . . hangings. . .* He was sure he heard his name. Skuli's too, and Emma's. There was another tremor and the air filled with yelps of delight. They crouched lower as a mob of children hurtled past. A whoop went up as a kid lit the petrol tank of another car and it burst into flames.

Jack signalled to Skuli and they drew back and went a different way, dodging the kids, keeping close to the twisted pine tree in the middle of the square. Jack bit his lip as they passed its gnarled trunk. Where there had been one noose swaying from the branch before, now there were three.

As they hurried on, Jack thought of something the monk had said to Tor, something Petter had said in the *kafé*. *The god of hanged men . . . sacrificial hangings . . . a favourite way to worship Odin.* He shuddered as he remembered the tree of dangling bodies carved on the standing stone.

Fireworks exploded nearby and there were shouts and laughter and scars of light streaked across the sky. Jack and Skuli used the distraction to slip away.

They ran up the lane and reached the church, panting. The pale gold sun lit the carvings on the door. Dragons prowled through tangled stems and twisted faces stared out from the shadows.

Sno pressed round Jack's legs. "Stay, Sno!" Jack hissed. He took hold of the heavy ring handle. "Once we're in," he said to Skuli, "you get out of sight. If something goes wrong. . ." – he swallowed and pressed a hand to his pocket, feeling the fake arrowhead there – "just be ready in case we need the runes."

Skuli shook his head. "I meant to tell you. I checked them when we saw those kids." He pulled up his sleeve and showed Jack an arm.

And Jack saw now how faded the ravens' marks were; nothing more than faint scabby lines. The protection runes were as good as gone.

He took a breath, then slowly turned the metal handle and eased the door open.

20
THE STAVE CHURCH

Full long let he look about him
For little he knows where a foe may lurk,
And sit in the seats within.

THE HÁVAMÁL

Cold air brushed Jack's cheek as he stepped into the church. There was the smell of damp wood and dead candle wax. His shadow stretched down the aisle from the open door. Out of the corner of his eye he watched Skuli slip into a dark space between the benches.

Jack walked up the aisle. Light slanted in from small windows high up the walls and lay in pools along the strip of blood-red carpet. Wooden beams emerged from the tops of the soaring wooden pillars; ornately carved balconies towered in stacks towards the roof. Eyes watched him from long-dead faces; faded paintings inside mottled gold frames. There was a distant bang as a firework exploded somewhere outside, muffled by the church's thick timber walls, then the only sound was his shallow breathing and his slow footsteps.

Jack reached the centre of the church. Still there was no one, nothing. Was he too late? As he took a breath, a sick feeling was drawn up from his belly to his throat. Ahead of him in the murk he made out the altar: a wooden slab table carved with ornate crosses and some kind of coiled dragon. His body tensed as a tremor rumbled through the soles of his shoes. A prayer book toppled from a bench on to the floor and he heard the dull clang of the bell high in the church tower.

The silence returned, pressing in on Jack, slowing his progress even more. He passed the benches nearest the altar and stopped. Shivers rippled over his skin and it took him a few seconds to realize what he was looking at, wrapped in white cloth and laid out on the long wooden seats. Three bodies.

He remembered the people killed in the plague of air. They had been brought here. Shoulders hunched, he stared at the corpses, feeling his confidence trickling away. Where was Emma? What if it was obvious the arrowhead was a fake?

"Do you have it?"

Jack felt his flesh crawl. Vekell's voice echoed eerily towards him from the direction of the altar.

"Where's Emma?" Jack spoke loudly, pushing the fear away. He stepped forward but still couldn't make out Vekell. "I want to see Emma first."

Vekell appeared to one side of the altar, his shadowy face unreadable. He pulled Emma into view and she gasped as she saw Jack.

"What are you *doing* here?"

Jack saw that her hands and arms were bound, her legs tied with twisted loops knotted round one side of the altar. There was a bruise across her face.

"You shouldn't have come! You have to burn the arrowhead!" She struggled against her ropes.

Jack said nothing. He resisted the urge to dive forward, punch Vekell and untie Emma. She was OK, he told himself. She was alive. He took a small step forward.

"Stop!" said Vekell. Jack saw metal glint by Emma's throat. "Show it to me."

Slowly Jack opened his fingers and let Vekell see the arrowhead in his palm. Emma gave a choked cry. "Jack! What are you doing?"

"Throw it to me."

Jack felt hot prickles in his chest. "Step away from Emma first," he heard himself say. "Slide the axe towards me."

A thin smile appeared on Vekell's face, like he saw right through Jack, like he totally knew how feeble he was feeling, but he moved away from Emma and slung the axe along the floor.

Somehow Jack managed not to flinch. There was a jarring clang as it slid to a stop beside him.

"Now," said Vekell. A cold impatience in his voice amplified across the high wooden beams of the church. "Throw what *you* have to *me*."

He's going to know. Jack's breathing sped up. The runes were all reversed! He imagined Skuli making his way through the church, slipping soundlessly between the benches. Jack pressed down on the axe with a foot. If things turned nasty, would he be willing to use it?

"Throw it to me!" demanded Vekell.

"No, Jack," Emma shouted. "You can't!"

Jack tossed the arrowhead and Vekell caught it in his fist and lowered his head to study it.

He's bound to guess. Did we really think we could fool him?

Vekell's forehead creased as he turned the arrowhead over.

Slowly Jack lowered his arm, fingertips twitching, reaching for the axe. *Be ready.*

Emma's voice became a thin wail that seemed to spiral up the height of the church. "Jack, what have you *done*?" It was so full of despair that even Vekell looked up from the gold a moment. And in that tiny instant Jack saw – or thought he saw – close to the glass of a high window, the fleeting shape of a raven. . .

Vekell's face relaxed. He closed his fist round the arrowhead. Then he swept past Jack down the aisle, his fur cloak brushing Jack's face as he went past. Out of the church the man went, like they no longer existed.

Jack launched himself up the steps of the altar with the axe, pulling at Emma's ropes, jabbing with the axe blade to try and sever the fibres without cutting her.

Her voice was hoarse when she finally spoke. "You should have had the funeral without me. Now we're all dead. *Everyone!*"

Skuli appeared beside them and held out his hand to

Emma. Before she had time to react, he pressed the arrow-head against a piece of rope and it fell away instantly.

"*What?*" She stared in disbelief. "But how. . ."

"We made a copy," said Skuli quietly, continuing the cutting.

Emma gave a cracked laugh. "We still have it! We can still do this! I thought. . ." Her hands came free and she rubbed at the red lines on her wrists. Her voice wobbled with emotion. "I thought you should have carried on without me."

Jack looked at her, then looked away. His throat went tight so the words came out all gruff. "Did you think we could?"

Emma pulled them into an awkward hug, then quickly brushed a tear from her face. "Get the rest of these ropes off me, then!" she said with a half smile. "What's with the Viking outfits?"

"We've got some clothes for you too," said Jack, and Skuli held up a baggy tunic. "The kids are searching for us. And there's no more protection runes."

Emma's smile faded. "There was a big gang of kids at the end of Church Lane when I was coming up here. That's why I followed Plan B and went straight to the museum."

"You keep the arrowhead for now, Skuli." Jack put down the axe and used his teeth to untie the last of the knots. Emma wriggled her legs free, then pulled the tunic over her head. Together they ran down the aisle.

"We got to the museum and then . . ." Jack frowned as

they reached the door. "We left it open." He fumbled around in the shadows for the handle and lifted the heavy ring of metal. It didn't turn. He tried forcing it the other way, then rattled it in confusion.

"What's going on?" said Emma, having a go and then giving the door a hard kick.

Jack pressed an ear to the wood. "Shhh!"

On the other side he heard a sound like liquid being splashed. A pungent smell wafted through the keyhole. *Petrol?*

Jack rammed against the door with his shoulder. Skuli and Emma joined in, but it still didn't budge. Jack stared through the keyhole again. He saw a small flare of fire, Vekell's face caught briefly in its light, then the wood went warm against his hand.

He drew back in shock as black smoke seeped from the thin gap at the bottom of the door. Dark patches appeared on the surface. Flames curled under the door, climbing quickly round the frame, making the wood fizz and spit. The carved lattice over the door caught and the fire fanned up the wall. For a few seconds, the speed of its spreading seemed to mesmerize Jack. He stood watching the bank of flames rise and come nearer, listening to the creaking whine of ancient timber heating and splitting.

"We need to find another way out!" he shouted, and they ran back through the church to the side door, the three of them wrenching the handle, hammering and kicking at it.

Jack looked back at the entrance and saw only fire. At

least Sno should have had the sense to get away, right? Two of the wooden pillars were sheer flame. A blazing line moved like a crack along the wall and a bench caught light.

"I'm pretty sure this is the only other exit!" gasped Skuli. He threw himself against it.

Emma dragged a bench towards them. "Use this to try and break the door down!"

They hoisted the bench up. "One, two, three!" cried Jack, and they heaved it forward. Again. Again. But the ramming hardly dented the surface. The heavy door was locked tight.

"The axe!" There was the sound of shattering glass as a window exploded. Jack's face prickled even at that distance, and the acrid smell hit the back of his throat, making his eyes stream. The smoke was already at waist height and rising. *No time!*

They abandoned the door and ran through an archway into a side alcove, but all they found were priests' clothes, hanging from metal rails like headless people.

"Here, look!" Skuli tugged at a black curtain, revealing a low doorway. Behind it Jack saw triangular lines of wooden steps zigzagging up and up a narrow shaft, then disappearing into shadow.

"The bell tower," wheezed Skuli, his face glazed with sweat. "I went up there once. There are windows at the top that open onto the roof, but—"

From behind them came the roaring hiss of flames and the thud of tumbling beams. Sparks sprayed through the air, sizzling holes in the fabric of the curtain. There was no time to think as they tore through the low door and pelted up the steps. No time to talk things through. No way back. No way to realize they were climbing straight into a death trap.

21

NO ESCAPE

The fire raged,
The earth was rocked.
VÖLSUNGA SAGA

Jack sprang upwards, feeling the vibration in the staircase as the others pounded after him. His hand skimmed the rusty railing, hardly touching the flimsy metal. Glancing down, he saw smoke rising in a dense column.

"Faster!" he yelled to the others. What had Skuli said? *Windows at the top that open on to the roof.*

The tower narrowed, the stairs becoming shorter and steeper as they got higher. Finally they reached a narrow balcony. There were no more steps, only wooden struts fixed in a spiral above them.

"See the windows?"

Skuli pointed and Jack spotted circles of glass overhead like gaping mouths.

"We'll have to climb up to them. You first, Emma." Jack

hoisted her up, then Skuli. "*Go!*"

Smoke surged up over Jack as he searched for footholds, using the angled planks as a freakish ladder. A strut snapped and his foot dangled helplessly. He'd bitten his tongue and he tasted blood between his teeth. He thought of Tor as he kicked about and finally found a grip. With a grunt, he hoisted himself up, moving as fast as his throbbing muscles would let him. Faster than they would let him.

But the slip had lost him precious seconds. A dense smell of burning stung his throat, and it was painful when he swallowed. He saw the bell above him. Wisps of smoke slithered up its black surface and gushed out through an opening. Jack struggled to see. His eyes watered painfully. Sweat slid down his face, stinging his lids. There was a rising draught of heat. He could hear crashing sounds below, a tearing growl, and now there were spiky flames beneath him, reaching up through the smoke.

"Skuli?" he called, breaking into a fit of coughing. "Emma?" He couldn't see them. He struggled for breath in the toxic air. If he made it to a window without falling, what then? Did it really open on to the roof? And even if it did. . . He wedged himself between two struts, desperation growing.

Another tremor started. Jack's Viking helmet slipped from his head, and he watched it plunge down the shaft. He gripped the shuddering wood strips tight, his arms and legs burning with the effort.

The bell rang. An explosion of sound vibrated right through Jack as he clung there, wincing at the noise, trying not to think about the tower collapsing; trying not to think about falling into that pit of flames at the bottom of the shaft.

The clanging slowed. Jack levered himself up, his vision blurred in the suffocating smoke, his breathing quick and shallow. His lungs felt like they were turning to cement. He reached up and his fingers curled over a jutting ledge. He gritted his teeth and forced his other hand up to grip it. He prised himself up with his elbows.

Then all at once hands were pulling him. He was hoisted up and then slipped forward on his stomach.

There was a shock of fresher air. He gulped oxygen into his body. A breeze cooled his face as he rested it against a steeply sloping roof. He saw wood tiles stretching away, the ground a long way down, and beyond them black clouds billowing over the carved crosses and dragon heads. Skuli and Emma sat slumped and panting.

Jack lurched to his feet. "*Go on!*" he wheezed at them. "Get up!" He gripped Emma's hand to pull her to her feet. "We have to get off this roof!"

Taking scuttling sideways steps, he set off. Heat radiated through the tiles. *Not too fast,* he warned himself, steadying his feet against the gradient. *You'll be straight over the edge!*

But now he saw metallic ribbons of fire stretching across nearby sections of the church roofs. One of them collapsed, giving way to leaping clusters of flame. Thick smoke poured from the bell tower. Gleaming ash spun through the air, raining down on to them. The burning church, a beacon on the hill. You'd see it for miles. Jack thought about the kids and swallowed. *Sno will have got away, right?*

The sun was approaching the horizon, its gold light merging with the sparks and floating embers, and that strange bank of cloud was still oozing round the peak of the mountain. It seemed denser now, threads of coloured light sparking through. What *was* that? Jack wondered.

The roof ended and they wobbled on the brink. Jack looked down. It was still a long way to the ground; too far to jump, not without doing serious damage. So much for the useless ravens. Where were they when you needed them? He pressed one foot experimentally on the guttering, but its brittle rusted joints snapped and a whole section came away.

Jack licked his cracked lips, his chest heaving. So shinning down the drainpipe wasn't an option. . . What now? Jump and hope they didn't break too many bones? The bottom of his boots felt tacky against the wood beam that bordered the roof. The smell of melting rubber mixed with the bitter fumes of the fire. His fingers raked his hair. Soon there wouldn't be any other option; no other choice but to jump, fall.

Emma's eyes scanned round wildly and she tugged at Jack's arm. "The flag pole?"

Skuli shook his head. "Too far."

But Jack stared across at the smooth tapering rod with rope twanging against it. The flag twitched at the top, the emblem of Isdal peppered with burn marks from the hot ash; its blue sea background; its gold sun; its two black birds with spread wings. "So there you are, ravens," he muttered.

He leaned out as far as he dared, almost touching the edge of the flag. Almost. And with a bit of a run-up, a lucky grab on the rope. . . Jack measured the distance mentally. If he could do it, the others would know to follow and he could try and get a hold of them when they jumped and. . .

A section of roof nearer to them collapsed with a roar, and Skuli gave a cry.

A silly, nervy commentary started running through Jack's mind. He couldn't stop it. *And so we come to the final penalty of this gruelling shoot-out.* He went back up the roof as far as he dared. There was no time to wonder if the pole would take his weight; one thing he knew for sure was that the roof wouldn't do so much longer.

If Tomassen can save this, the title of world champions will be theirs. If not. . .

He turned. *Tomassen's in the box, never once taking his eyes off the ball . . . The striker SHOOTS. . .*

He ran full pelt down the roof, forcing out a bellowing cry to drive himself on.

Tomassen dives. . .

He got to the edge and vaulted forward, and then he was reaching with arms stretched. Reaching . . . Further, further. . .

Time slowed down. Jack arched over the gap of air. His body extended as if it was about to snap. There was the brief feeling of flying, then the tug of gravity. His fingers strained and clutched for the flag rope.

His chest smacked the pole, crushing the air out of his lungs. White light burst across his skull. His insides were being rattled, like coins in a moneybox. But he was on the flag pole! His arms and legs wrapped tightly round it, his heart thumping against the slippery painted surface, the rope balled round his fist.

And the crowd goes wild! Tomassen's saved it! Unbelievable!

The spooling commentary evaporated as Jack became aware of a hissing sound nearby. He looked up to see fire sweeping greedily over the roof. "Come on!" he shouted to Skuli and Emma. His throat felt like it had razor blades crammed in it. With a cry of effort, he pulled himself straight, rotating his ankle to get his foot in a solid loop of rope. Then he leaned into the gap, his arms outstretched.

Emma took a run-up. She lunged towards him and there was a wrenching impact. He clung on to her, his arms almost torn out of their sockets. Her nails dug into his skin. There was a splitting sound as a crack widened along the pole.

"Get down!" Jack said, jaw still vibrating, and quickly she was shinning down the pole, sliding down the last stretch to the ground. Jack let out a sharp breath. "You now, Skuli!"

Skuli blinked towards him, sweat streaming down his sooty face as he broke into a sprint. Jack saw the tiles disintegrate beneath his feet as his friend ran forward, the roof collapsing, crumbling as he jumped, his Viking helmet whizzing away. He slammed into the pole so hard that Jack was knocked right off it.

Pain wrenched through Jack's leg as the rope looped round his foot swung violently outwards. He heard barking from somewhere below; saw the flag alight, the ravens in flames. As he hurtled back towards the flagpole, Skuli slid past him on his way down, mouth wide.

Jack grabbed the pole and spiralled round it, following. His knees buckled as he landed at the base. He rolled over the grass and lay there as his friends crouched over him, Sno giving him slobbery licks.

"Thanks, Skuli," Jack croaked, patting his dog with a stiff hand. "I always wanted to try the fireman's pole."

Skuli gave a wry smile, then used the arrowhead to slice the rope from Jack's foot. Emma helped him to sit. "God, look at the sun." She glanced at her watch and cried out in horror. "There's hardly an hour until midnight! We've got to get to Tor."

Jack broke into a limping run. They skirted the engulfed church, shielding their faces from the heat, aiming for the lane on the other side of the hill.

But then Jack grabbed Skuli and Emma's arms and they skidded to a stop. "Wait!" He rubbed his still-stinging eyes. "I saw something."

He grabbed hold of Sno and they rushed for cover, crouching behind a gravestone with outstretched angel wings. Scraggly bushes covered the ground nearby, and Jack slid forward on his stomach, straining to see through the thorny branches. The back of his neck was moist with sweat.

Hooded figures moved in front of the blaze. He counted five, six, but more appeared every second. "Kids!" he whispered. They'd obviously seen the fire.

Just now the kids were doing something weird. They

had all stopped and turned in the direction of the sun. It was like they sensed something; the moment getting closer. Their faces glinted, reflecting the sunlight, and Jack realized that they were wearing masks: expressionless gold-coloured masks that covered just their eyes and noses.

A chant thumped the air, getting louder and faster as more voices joined in.

"*Odin's vengeance. Hunt. Kill. Our god must have his sacrifice.*

Odin's vengeance. Hunt. Kill. Our god must have his sacrifice."

Jack heard a voice rise above the others. It sounded like Lukas, but with the hoods and masks there was no way to be sure. The kids seemed to merge, locking into a procession that snaked and seethed as they chanted.

Skuli edged out from behind the gravestone but Jack shot out a hand to stop him. "*No!*" he hissed. "Wait till I say!"

The ground beneath them shuddered with another tremor, and Jack heard screams of delight and the wild clanging of the bell in the burning tower. The plague of earth, building up to something big.

The procession wound down the lane and Jack saw their chance. He tugged the hood of his tunic over his head and gestured to Skuli and Emma to do the same.

"Now!" The three of them moved fast, away from the graveyard and downhill, through the close-packed, spindly trees. Branches whipped Jack's skin as he dodged the branches, keeping Skuli and Emma close. They skirted round thorny hollows and stumbled on patches of bare ground. How much further? wondered Jack, half running, half tumbling over the rough ground. He struggled to get a sense of the direction as they moved faster and faster. . .

And then, without warning, they were somehow on the gravel of the lane.

Right in the thick of the procession.

Jack's legs scrambled on the loose surface. He stopped dead. The kids were all around them. It was too late to draw back; too late to hide.

"Be part of it!" hissed Emma. She waved her arms, copying their swaying dance.

The kids surged round them as Jack and Skuli joined in, Sno weaving round their legs. The four of them continued down the lane, deliberately slowly so the kids swept past and tramped on ahead.

Jack felt a tug at his tunic. Then another. "Skuli," he hissed. "*What?*"

But it wasn't Skuli. When he turned he saw a small girl, staring up at him, biting the ends of her hair under her mask. Jack saw Skuli's look of panic, Emma shaking her head. "You're Jack," the small girl said. "They want to get you."

"I'm not Jack. I'm Jon. Have a sweet." Jack fumbled in his pocket, desperate to distract her.

"You *are* Jack," she said. "I'm not *stupid*. That's your dog."

"Here. Look." Thank god for chocolates, even if they were melted into a clump. "Want one?" He stifled the urge to clamp a hand over that silly little mouth. Shut her up.

The small girl chewed the mangled mess, licking her

blue lips, but kept on staring.

"Oh, look," Jack said, pointing behind her. "Your mummy and daddy have woken up."

"Where?" she said suspiciously, whirling round and lifting herself up on tiptoes. "Where?"

"Just over there," said Jack. "Can't you see them?"

They edged away, the little girl still peering up the lane.

We're almost clear. Jack kept close to Emma and Skuli as they headed for the cover of the trees. *Just a few more steps. . .*

"*Jaaaaaack!*" the savage shout went up.

The girl was loud for such a small one, he'd give her that, and the fact she was pointing straight at him didn't help. The procession stopped. One by one, in a ripple of movement, the masked faces turned to look.

"Run," said Jack out of the side of his mouth. His legs started to pound the ground before his brain could properly kick in.

There were shouts and the kids started running too, and then a cry went up, even louder then before. Only this time it came from Jack himself. "*Run!*"

22

MASKS

What is twisted cannot be straightened.
ECCLESIASTES 1:15

Jack ran, and the mob followed. *Get away!* he shouted inside his head. *Get to Tor.*

Then there was no room for any other thinking, just trying to see the way ahead; trying to get enough breath; just the mass of masked kids streaming behind like they were one single thing.

It wasn't until they reached the square that the next tremor hit.

But instead of fading away, this tremor was followed by another, stronger one that forced them to the ground. Debris rained down from buildings. Roof tiles crashed on to the road. Cracks appeared in the tarmac and up the sides of buildings. There was the groan of shifting timber. Jack saw walls buckle and slump, straining to stay upright;

collapsing in on themselves.

As he struggled to his feet he made out Gran and Gramps's house. Thank god that was still standing. Then he heard the short laughing screams of the mob and there was nothing to do but run on.

"The footbridge!" Jack shouted as they neared the river. A wild, desperate plan spun through his mind. It was the only way to the museum. If they could get across to the other side without being caught. . .

The narrow suspension bridge trembled as they started across it, Skuli first, then Emma, then Jack, leaping the gaps and the jagged slats of broken wood. They were almost on the other side when Skuli stopped with a cry and Jack slammed into Emma as they bunched up behind.

There was a masked boy at the end of the bridge. He must have somehow raced ahead. Tall, wide shoulders. Lukas? He stood there, blocking the walkway, and Jack saw now that he was holding a knife: a long-bladed knife with a jagged edge, the kind that hunters used.

Jack spun round to see the mob stopped at the other end of the bridge. Sno was hunched, teeth bared and growling, and the kids watched from behind their expressionless gold masks.

A whisper went up. "*Hang them from the bridge! Yes! From the bridge!*" The words hissed through the crowd, and Jack saw three kids near the front, each holding something stretched between their fists.

Three lengths of rope. Three nooses.

The bridge juddered as one of the kids stepped on to it.

Before Jack could react, there was a yell, and he turned to see Skuli shoot forward, ramming headlong into the boy with the knife, knocking him backwards off the bridge. The blade spun on to the ground, but the boy was up again in an instant. He gave a violent punch to Skuli's head, and Skuli fell hard against the twisted steel of a suspension cable driven into the ground.

As the boy reached for the weapon, Jack saw Emma spring off the footbridge and kick it back on to the walkway. He smacked her in the face. She rolled across the ground, and he darted past her to retrieve it.

Jack felt the suspension bridge sway as the mob poured on from the other side. He flung a fist at the first masked face and the kid fell back, but the next loomed up instantly, and more were coming all the time, packing on to the walkway, trapping Jack between them and the boy with the knife.

Sno snarled and barked, biting at fingers. Jack saw his jaw clamp round a wrist. But there were so many kids, kicking and trampling, blue mouths shouting. Too many of them.

I'm not going to make it. I'll never get off this bridge.

He saw Emma crawling to her feet, one eye half shut and bloody. Skuli was gripping the cable, dragging himself up.

The desperate idea flashed again into Jack's mind as he hit out and was punched back. The one slim chance they had. Emma and Skuli were off the bridge . . . Skuli had the arrowhead. . .

Sno leapt up, teeth snapping savagely. As the mob

swayed back from his bites, it gave Jack the space he needed. He gathered his strength to shout:

"Skuli! Cut the cables!"

Emma's mouth dropped and Skuli shook his head violently, but Jack's voice rose, commanding. "*Do it! You can launch the boat without me!*"

"The bridge is going down!" he yelled at the mob as they surged over Sno. Fingers grabbed his throat; rough hands tried to slip a rope round his neck. Through a sea of thumping arms, he saw Skuli, face creased with indecision, arrowhead raised over the cable. The boy was charging back along the walkway with his knife, eyes fixed on the gold. Jack braced himself. What choice did Skuli have? *Cut the cable!*

The walkway lurched. The punches stopped as kids staggered back. Jack clung to the steel wire running by his feet as each shake came stronger than the last; wave after powerful wave.

The bridge tilted like a boat capsizing. Jack saw the churning river below him as the walkway swung up at a sheer angle. Skuli was on his knees, the cable still uncut, the boy still on the bridge. . .

Rocks broke off the gorge and crashed towards the water. The kids streamed back off the bridge and scattered, falling over themselves in their haste. The surface shot up again and the boy slid towards Jack, giving him a vicious kick as he passed, then anchoring himself on the handrail.

Jack saw Sno crouched in the middle of the walkway, eyes wide, ears flat back. He crawled towards his dog, reaching forward between the jolts, grabbing a fistful of Sno's trembling fur and pulling him close.

The boy was clawing his way back towards them. Skuli and Emma were at the end of the bridge, lying on their stomachs over the gorge edge, reaching out. "Jack! Come on!"

Clutching Sno, Jack edged painfully towards them on all fours, slowly closing the gap. The walkway went into another spasm. His knee broke through a slat and he pressed his chest against the disintegrating surface, holding Sno tight. He tried to drag himself forward, but now one foot wouldn't move at all, and as he twisted to free it, he saw the boy with the knife had hold of his boot.

The suspension bridge rose up, almost vertically, then crashed down with a sickening wrench, setting off a rippling effect, like the movement of a snake. From the far side came a grating squeal of steel, and Jack saw the suspension cables wrench up from the ground, lurching free of their supports.

He gritted his teeth and held on to Sno. *This is it*, he told himself. *The bridge is going down.*

More planks fell, shaken out like rotten teeth. The grip on Jack's foot went slack. He kicked back hard and heaved himself forward over the rickety boards. But he felt himself slipping as the bridge buckled. *It's breaking loose on the other side!* Sno gave a yelping whimper, paws flailing. Jack fought to stop them both from falling.

"Reach for us!" he heard Skuli shout from above. "More! Just a bit more!"

Jack hoisted Sno up and pushed him forward.

"Now you, Jack!" screamed Emma. "Reach!"

Jack stretched until his bones seemed to snap. Their fingertips touched. The bridge was collapsing under him, his body sliding towards trembling ground. Hands held his wrists and wrenched him up. . .

But just below was the boy, his mask broken off and spiralling down into the gorge. Jack shot out a hand and grabbed hold of his wrist, as the last slab of bridge came away.

"Give me your other hand!" Jack held tight to the boy's fingers, gasping at the burning pain in his shoulder socket. "Your other hand. . ." he hissed between his teeth. "Please, Lukas."

Lukas dangled over the deep gorge, his wrist slowly slipping from Jack's fingers. *Why won't he listen?* thought Jack desperately. *Why won't he try and save himself?*

Lukas looked up, blinking with some kind of surprise, realization; and Jack saw that the blue colour was gone from his mouth. Their eyes locked. "Then we'd both fall," Lukas said, with a small, sad shake of his head.

It was the last thing Jack saw before it came, that one last quake that flung him and Sno, Skuli and Emma backwards across the cracking ground. That last awful plague of earth that sent the edge of the ravine crashing and crumbling and tumbling away.

23

LAUNCH

Wonder seized him, to know what
manner of men they were.

BEOWULF

Jack lay on his stomach, staring down at the river. But there was no sign of Lukas. No sign of the other fallen kids.

He crawled to his feet. His hands were bleeding, but he couldn't feel anything, just his teeth clamped shut; bile rising in his throat. Sno pushed against him, trembling.

Jack heard Skuli and Emma's shallow breathing as they helped him up. Beyond the ravine, masked children were getting to their feet as well and stood watching them.

His mind switched to Mum, Gran, Gramps, Emma's parents... He stared at the shattered bridge, hanging straight down into the gorge. There was no way back now.

And Tor's boat! Jack's breathing sped up. What might the big quake have done to that?

"I nearly cut that cable." Skuli's eyes were round with

shock. "If that earthquake hadn't come. . ." He blinked at the arrowhead lying by their feet.

Jack limped over and gave him a light punch on the arm. "I'd rather *you* kill me than *them*." Jack cast a wary eye at the still-motionless kids on the other side of the gorge. He held the arrowhead a moment, then placed it in his chest pocket. "Forget it. Come on!"

The three of them stumbled into a run, Sno lolloping ahead down the slanting track towards the water.

"And the plague of fire?" called Emma tensely.

In his mind, Jack saw the blank panel on the standing stone. What would the last plague be? He had no idea. But it was coming, and soon. His sore knees jarred as they descended the slope. The golden sun seemed to be expanding as it dropped, getting more intense each moment.

Twenty minutes.

They got to the water's edge and followed the boardwalk towards the museum, the sea lapping up on to the slippy wooden planks. Despite the strong sea air, Jack could smell burning, and when he glanced back he saw the church on the hill, still glowing bright against the sky.

And then there was the mountain. Something strange was happening with Brennbjerg. The metallic banks of cloud were thicker now, and swarmed and circled round its peak. Strange sparks of light flared from its rocky ridges. He swallowed and forced his eyes away from it; made himself concentrate on the job in hand.

Ahead of them was the museum. As they got closer, Jack saw that its steel walls had buckled and wide cracks were running up the concrete pillars.

They eased through the mangled door, framed with jagged glass. "Is it safe?" hissed Emma.

Safe from the roof falling in, did she mean? thought Jack as he stepped over a headless mannequin. Or from Vekell on the prowl? As long as that nutter thought he had the real arrowhead, he'd leave them alone, right? With a bit of luck he'd be pinned under a massive slab of collapsed building somewhere.

But Jack couldn't help glancing behind him all the same.

They picked their way through the wrecked corridors strewn with rotten-smelling seaweed and broken ceiling tiles, keeping together, moving as fast as they dared.

Tor? The dragon ship? Jack dreaded what he'd find.

At last they stumbled through the narrow doorway of the boat gallery. A cold breeze stung Jack's face. The huge doors at the end of the room were hanging off their hinges, gaping open to the sea. The dragon boat glowed gold from the low sun streaming in. It was still sitting in its metal cradle. At least that was something.

"No need to worry about smashing the glass to get it out, after all," Jack said with a tight smile.

"And Tor?" said Emma anxiously. "Can I see him?"

Jack rushed to the boat, and there was the body, lying as if newly asleep, untouched by the earthquakes. He sank over the edge of the hull with relief.

He heard Emma catch her breath beside him. "He really is so like you, Jack." She fingered her archery bow and arrows in the hull, unable to take her eyes away from Tor's face.

"I really thought the quake would have done more harm," said Skuli. "Might the ravens have helped? Protected him or something? The rest of the room's pretty messed up."

Jack shrugged impatiently. "Well, they weren't giving *us* much help, so you might be right." But there was no time to think about those ravens now. The sun's light reflected in the water, as if the bay was full of lava, and Jack's heart raced as he checked his watch.

Fifteen minutes.

He inspected the pair of lighters; and the firelighters, all neatly laid out along the hull. The runes on his arms prickled and he rubbed hard at the sore skin. He saw that the wheels of the boat cradle were still sitting on their rails. Quickly he checked along their length, the three of them stooping hurriedly to clear the debris. "The metal's got warped in places," Jack said. "See that?" Sliding the boat straight out and into the water wasn't going to be that simple any more.

He stood beneath the rope dangling from a pulley in the cracked ceiling. "All grab this! Pull on three! One . . . two . . . three . . . *pull!*"

Jack felt the resistance of the wheels against the rails as they heaved on the rope. The pulleys above them jerked tight. There was the squeal of metal against metal. "*Pull!*"

"*More!*" Skuli grunted beside him. Jack's feet scrambled against the floor. But the boat didn't budge.

Thirteen minutes.

Emma was staring out at the bay. She took a slight step

forward. Jack wiped his face with his arm. "What is it?"

"I thought I heard something." She pointed vaguely at the sky. "Out there."

Jack glanced up nervously. The air was quiet. Too quiet. Not even the sound of lapping waves. Above them were the same weird metallic clouds he'd seen over the mountain, but spreading across the sky now, fusing with the dense gold of the approaching sunset.

Jack straightened and shielded his eyes as he spotted something. Two birds circling. The ravens! With slow beats of their wings, they glided down, then rose again and continued to loop.

Jack tightened his grip on the rope, wrapping it a couple of times round his wrist. "Try again!" he ordered, his voice thick. "Pull harder!"

The sun was a molten disc now, boring into their eyes so they could hardly see. Once it was touching the horizon, how long did they have until it began to climb again? Three minutes, maybe four? That was all. That would be the moment, the zero moment, with the sun refusing to set; day refusing to give in to night.

Sweat ran down Jack's face and neck. His fingernails dug into his palms. After everything they'd been through! They'd got this far; they'd got so close! He wasn't going to give in. He'd made a promise to Skuli that he'd help him put things right! They had to save the town!

He sprang over to the boat and gripped the edge of the hull. "*Pull!*" he shouted at his friends, and as they strained back with the rope, he pushed, ramming and rocking his whole body against the solid wooden hull. Pain shot along his shoulders and back. His feet scrambled against the floor, leg muscles burning. . .

Eleven minutes.

And then, just when Jack thought he couldn't push any more, ever so slightly, the boat shifted.

"*Yes!*" Emma cried out. "Keep it going!"

"More!" panted Skuli, his face red and glistening.

"Come *on!*" Jack shouted. The boat was starting to slide. *It was moving!* Gravity was taking over. If they could get it as far as the door. . .

Ten minutes.

"Nearly," said Skuli, his voice slurred with effort.

The dragon boat picked up speed. Shadows slithered over the coiled snakes along the dragon's neck; its eyes sparked and its sharp teeth glinted. *Our glorious chieftain,* the runes inside the open mouth shouted in Jack's mind. *Vekell the Great.*

Sno gave a whimper. He darted round Jack's feet, looking up at the prow, his ears pricked.

The boat got faster. "Get ready!" shouted Jack, breaking into a run.

The dragon boat slid down the sloping bank and into the water with an explosion of spray. As it came loose from the cradle, it levelled itself, then floated on the water, sail flapping loose. It drifted a little way, then the single thick rope holding it went taut, and there it stayed, gently rising and falling with the waves from the bay.

"Result!" screamed Emma, and Skuli gave a shouting

laugh.

Jack felt his face crack into a grin, but there was no time for celebrations. *Nine minutes.* He sprang on to the boat and crouched over Tor's body. He took a long, deep breath. It was time to put the arrowhead where Skuli had first found it. Time to return the arrowhead to Tor so he could carry it back to Odin.

Skuli gave a shout and, startled, Jack looked up at where he was pointing. The Brennbjerg mountain. The dense column of smoke rising from its peak. There was a burst of fiery sparks and, a fraction of a second later, the explosion shockwave pulsed out with an ear-splitting crack.

"The plague of fire!" Emma shouted, and they stared, hypnotized as metallic fountains arched over the mountain.

Eight minutes.

Jack tore his gaze away and knelt to press the arrowhead into Tor's hand. Somewhere close, a raven screeched. He scrambled to his feet and grabbed a lighter, tossing the other to Emma as she clambered onto the boat. Lava broke over the lip of the mountaintop and started to ooze down the slopes in a molten sheet. Globules exploded from the crater, raining down like fiery leaves.

He tried to steady himself on the rocking deck, rushing to light the first bundle of kindling.

And suddenly there was a figure standing on the rocks beside the boat.

24

DEATH BOAT

No keenest blade . . . could harm or hurt. . .
He was safe, by his spells, from sword of battle.

BEOWULF

Vekell held up the fake arrowhead and flung it at the water; then he looked at Jack. Beyond, the mountain erupted in molten jets. "I will return Odin's *real* gold to him and win the gods' favour," he snarled.

So that was it, thought Jack. Vekell wanted glory for himself. But it wouldn't work. It wasn't right! *Carried by warrior true of heart*, that's what the ballad said. Vekell wasn't true of heart! Tor was the one who'd shown true courage. He was the only one who could take the arrowhead.

The lava reached the mountain's lower slopes, a glowing river of rolling folds and sparks. It razed through a stretch of forest; trees burst into flame. Jack smelled the fumes. The smothering lava swept downwards, heading for the town.

Seven minutes.

Vekell drew a sword.

Sno sprang at the man, barking, but was knocked aside with a savage punch and lay still.

Jack gave a cry and Vekell's eyes fixed on him, pointing the tip of the blade. "Give me the arrowhead."

He can't see inside the boat from where he's standing, Jack told himself. *Think! Think!*

"*I've* got it," blurted Skuli, and in an instant Vekell swivelled towards him.

Jack heaved a shield from the deck and with a grunt of effort jumped from the boat as Vekell lunged at Skuli, the heavy metal disc glancing the man's back. Vekell stumbled to one side and Skuli rolled hard against the rocks, clutching his shoulder.

Vekell reeled round, sword edge shoving hard against the shield, making Jack smack to the ground, then continued to advance towards Skuli.

"I've got the arrowhead," Skuli said again defiantly, but this time his voice wavered. He limped backwards, gripping his shoulder.

Skuli! Jack got up, gasping for breath through his swollen mouth. He tried to reach his friend, but suddenly the ravens were in the way, huge wings spread and flapping, pushing him back towards the boat.

There was a swiping sound. An arrow rushing through the air. Vekell's sword was knocked from him and came to rest on the water's edge. He stood there, rocking slightly, caught off balance.

"*Emma*," whispered Jack, as he tried to crawl from

beneath the ravens' whirling feathers.

Emma's face was ghostly pale, her fingers trembling as she worked to set her next arrow. "We'll distract him," she hissed. "Go, Jack!"

Vekell was stepping over to retrieve his sword.

"*Jack!*" Emma slotted the arrow onto her bow and pulled the string taut. "*Go!*"

Jack stumbled to his feet, the ravens parting to make way for him.

Four minutes.

The sun was almost setting; a hovering blurred gold circle.

Jack jumped back on to the dragon boat and sprang over to Tor, to the bundles of kindling, fumbling with his lighter to get a flame.

The time must be now, the air seemed to whisper. The reek of lighter fuel filled his throat. Voices echoed across the water. *Light the boat!*

Three minutes.

Vekell was on his feet. Jack saw him make a run at Emma and she fell back hard, then scooped up his sword and strode towards Skuli. "The *arrowhead!*"

"*Skuli!*" panted Emma, trying to get back to her bow. Jack heard the sob in her voice as Vekell brought his sword towards Skuli's throat.

Jack gritted his teeth and looked away. What had Skuli said that time? *Sacrifice one to save all.*

He snatched the arrowhead from Tor's hands and held the gold high.

"Vekell!" he shouted, his bruised face throbbing. "I, Tor,

will be the one to return the arrowhead!"

He sliced down through the mooring rope; the strands fell away instantly, and he felt the tide tug the boat and the wind swirl inside the sail.

Vekell turned; slammed his sword into his scabbard. He charged towards the moving hull and made a staggering leap.

There was a splash and a jolt as Vekell latched on to the side of the hull. The boat lurched as he dragged himself aboard.

Jack pushed the arrowhead into his pocket and tried the lighter again. And once the boat was lit? There'd be no way back, except through the freezing water. He'd swim for it; he'd have to. He clicked the button, but there was nothing. He tried again, then shook the canister in a panic. There was plenty of gas, so what was the problem? Too damp to spark? He pressed harder. Vekell's wide shoulders came level with the top of the hull and he swung himself forward. *Come on!* Still nothing. Jack scanned the deck desperately for the second lighter, but there was no sign. Did Emma still have it?

Ravens circled overhead. The lava was flowing faster than ever down the mountainside. All that fire there and nothing here! Jack gave a desperate laugh as he tried with the lighter again and again. It was almost funny.

Jack felt the current catch, and the boat gathered speed, heading out into open water. He heard the helpless shouts of Skuli and Emma on the bank. He tried the lighter again. "*Come on!*" he pleaded.

Vekell landed heavily on the deck and slid out his sword.

There was a streak of movement and another of Emma's arrows whizzed wide of the boat. How many more did she have? Jack calculated. He felt his heartbeat in his throat. There'd been five. That left just two.

"The *arrowhead*!" Vekell came at him with the blade and Jack hurled himself across the deck as the metal sliced past. It smashed against the dragon's neck, sending up an explosion of jagged splinters. The lighter spun away from Jack's hand. At last a blue flame quivered on the end, but as he dived to grab it, it shot overboard, vanishing under the water.

Jack twisted to dodge Vekell's blows. Now there was no way to light the boat! No way to stop the plague of fire. It had all been for nothing.

Jack threw himself to one side as the sword jabbed forward, with such force that it embedded itself into the wood of the hull, Vekell grappling to release it.

Jack crouched beside Tor. He stared into his green eyes, and the dead boy's green eyes stared back at him. And in that moment, Jack decided something. Vekell wasn't going to get the arrowhead. Not after everything Jack had been through; that Tor had been through. At least he could fight to stop that!

Jack pressed the arrowhead into Tor's hands, closing the boy's fingers round it: gold on skin.

Then, with Vekell still trying to free his sword, Jack sprang at him, fastening on to the man's back, punching, gouging. Vekell gripped his shoulders, wrenching him to the ground; then a hand clamped on his throat, lifting him into the air.

Jack lashed out with his legs and fists. He couldn't draw breath. His head went light. Vaguely, he saw the ravens spiral overhead, and he didn't understand why they stayed like that, just watching, waiting. *Why won't you help me?*

Vekell had hold of something; the anchor chain? Its pitted surface scraped Jack's skin as it was wound round his neck.

Jack pulled at the metal links, gasping. Somewhere from across the water came shouting. *Emma? Skuli?* He saw a streak of light in the sky. An arrow? Jack's eyes widened as he watched it coming. The chain slackened a little, as Vekell must have seen it too. The flight was on fire! *Clever Emma! Clever Skuli! Aim for the sail!*

But the arrow lost height too fast and fell short of the boat and was gone, the flame blotted out instantly by the water.

The chain tightened. "Skuli," Jack murmured. "Emma." Then there was no more breath to speak. He was slipping; falling out of consciousness as he was lifted level with the dragon's mouth; held up against its teeth and snaking tongue and runes. *Vekell the Great. . . Vekell the Great. . .* His arms and legs went slack; his eyelids closed.

"Fight gone out of you, little brother?" Jack felt Vekell's words on his face as he spoke. He heard that familiar mocking lilt.

And suddenly, fleetingly, Jack was seeing as Tor again. He was on the dragon boat as it neared the monastery, dawn light catching on swords and domed helmets. But there was just him now, him and Vekell. Tor and Vekell.

"Only a warrior could take Odin's arrowhead back to him." Vekell's mouth was by his ear. "But you always were weak, little Tor. You always were a coward."

Coward? From somewhere deep inside him some last thing snapped, reacted. He saw Tor: making his promise to the dying monk; choosing to fall instead of giving Vekell the arrowhead; sacrificing himself to stop the plagues Tor in the ice cave, horribly wounded, alone and dying, carving his warning. *Coward?* Jack's eyes quivered open. Tor had given up the one thing he had left to give.

Was that the sacrifice Odin wanted?

Jack's blood pulsed faster, a clotting knot of anger. He closed his hand around the arrowhead. He didn't feel pain any more, only the pressure of his rage like a valve about to crack.

Is this what you want? his mind shouted.

Jack stabbed with the arrowhead. He felt the point meet flesh. The chain went loose and he slammed down against the wooden deck.

Warrior, the ravens murmured. Feathers brushed Jack's face. *Warrior of true heart.* The dragon's head swung into focus, and as the lava fumed and sparked beyond, it was as if the fanged mouth was spewing fire.

Jack never saw Emma shoot that final arrow.

He never even heard it coming.

He only saw it moving through the sky as he stared up, chest heaving, cradling the gold. For those few strange seconds he was mesmerized as he watched it arch in front of the erupting mountain, leaving a brilliant trail that lingered in the air. On it swept, over the water towards the boat, reaching its highest point then starting a long, curved descent.

Jack saw the arrow strike the sail and the fabric catch. He saw Vekell stagger from the heat, bleeding at the shoulder. He saw the fire drip like molten lava on to the prow, setting light to the oily bundles of kindling.

Fire swept up the inside of the hull. Petals along the hull crinkled and pine branches flared. Flames spiralled up the mast and climbed the dragon's neck.

"Jump, Jack!" Skuli bellowed across the water.

But Vekell had seen the arrowhead now, and he sprang towards Tor to snatch it, not seeing the length of anchor chain coiled across the deck. Jack saw him trip and sprawl, one leg snared, wrenching the chain, making the anchor unhook from its snake-shaped clasp on the side of the hull, making the heavy iron plunge into the deep, deep water.

Vekell crashed on to his chest, then his body was being dragged backwards as the anchor chain followed. His fingers clawed the deck as he was pulled towards the burning edge of the boat. As Jack stumbled up he felt Vekell's hand grip his ankle, tight like talons, making him slam again on to his back, sliding after Vekell.

Jack kicked and writhed against the man's impossible grip. He felt the heat increase. His arms swept in frantic arcs, fingers desperate to get a hold on something, anything.

A tree branch; fallen from the hull; one end in flames. Back curved painfully, Jack swiped it up, then down. . .

Right down on to Vekell's hand, fire on skin. Jack felt the fingers spring open; his leg released.

Jack scrambled back from the heat, coughing, eyes streaming.

He could only watch as Vekell was pulled over the edge of the hull, through the flames and into the water, disappearing below the waves. There was a hot slap of ashy air and Jack shook himself back into action. He saw the sun touching the horizon; the lava reaching for the buildings at the edge of the town. He laid his hands on Tor's one last time, feeling the pure gold spearhead there, exquisitely sharp.

Get off the boat!

He looked over the side at the moving water, at the waves slapping the hull. The ragged black sail flapped back and forth. A sheet of flames came at him and as the blast of heat hit . . .

he jumped.

25
FUNERAL

*The wisest alive can't tell
where a death ship goes.*
BEOWULF

Like falling through ice. Head first, headlong, through the water. The shock of it made Jack's chest seize up; his muscles tightened as he tried to thrash his arms and claw his way back towards the light.

His head broke the surface and he let out a great heaving gasp. Swatting water from his eyes, he saw more lava spew from the crater. He saw the flow still rolling forward, widening and accelerating, smothering the first houses.

His insides shrank. Why hadn't the eruption stopped? Hadn't the fire reached the arrowhead yet? The round sun hovered on the horizon, a disc on the edge of the world. He spun in the freezing water and looked at the boat as the flames rose higher. Had he been too late?

Jack treaded water, the heat on his face, the cold depths

taking hold of the rest of him. *It can't have all been for nothing!* He watched an edge of lava reach the shore, breaking over the rocks in thick metallic waves. There was a violent hiss of steam as the lava met the water and made it boil. A fiery flood spread along the side of the bay towards the museum.

Skuli! Emma! Sno! Jack shook himself from his daze and kicked towards shore. He was going to get back to them; stay together till the end of all this. But already the biting cold was draining his energy. He sliced with his arms across the gold-skinned water, but his movements slowed, his sodden clothes dragging him down.

All that lava, all that fire! Jack gave a spluttering laugh. Yet he'd freeze to death. Like Tor.

Like Dad.

Jack's head jerked up. *No!* He thrashed the water, gasping. Began one last impossible fight to get to the shore.

And now, above the cold water, there were strange, thin layers of warmth; currents from the lava gone into the bay. Jack's muscles pulsed with blood as the feeling returned to his legs.

He could see Emma on the bank, shouting as he swam. He felt a surge of heat on the back of his head and looked back to see the dragon boat flare. An intense light rose from the hull, a pillar of fire.

He stopped swimming.

There was a figure standing in the boat; a boy, tall, holding up the arrowhead.

"Tor," whispered Jack.

The heat made the air shudder. The gold in Tor's hand was a brilliant blade of light. Across the water, Jack saw a double sun, one reflecting a perfect twin, fused in strange symmetry; between them, the red horizon like a line of blood.

And then the twins were pulling away from each other, separating, and the sun began to rise.

The mountain poured smoke and the plumes of ash mixed with dazzling gold clouds, so bright that Jack had to shield his eyes. Through the swirling clouds, he thought he glimpsed a face, an old man's face. *Odin?* He extended his hand towards Tor, and then the two were gone.

The molten stream slowed to a stop. Ragged lava sizzled at the edge of the water, but came no nearer.

Jack gave a stifled laugh. *They'd done it! Had they really done it?* He found his stroke in the warmed water. He got to shore, and Skuli and Emma dragged him on to the rocky bank. The three huddled close, Sno resting his head on Jack's knees.

The boat was a glowing crescent. Sparks spiralled into the dawn sky. Jack looked for Tor, but he was gone. Ash fell round them like fine, black feathers. The funeral flames merged with the gold of the water, and the sky and the light on the land, and Jack gave a long breath out as the words of the ballad came to him.

For when fire, water, air, earth unite
In the light of a midnight sun,
The curse is broke; the gold is freed

The evil is undone.

"Look!" Emma pointed at the sky. "The ravens!"

The birds circled in the air like smoke, swooping closer.

"*Friend or foe, the demon birds,*" Skuli muttered.

The old monk's voice ran through Jack's mind. *The ravens have their own plan perhaps. . . One that is not Odin's.*

With soft caws, the ravens circled over them one more time, then flew towards the boat. Without slowing they swept straight into the funeral flames, and vanished.

Skuli straightened. "I know how the ballad ends," he said quietly, his gaze far away, his face glowing in the light from the blazing boat. And he recited the words as if he'd known them all along.

> "*That midsummer night was kinship forged*
> *'Tween daemons and warriors Three,*
> *And through the power of the funeral fire*
> *From their master's bonds fly free.*"

Jack nodded a little as understanding came to him. The arrowhead had been freed through fire. Now it was the ravens' turn to free themselves. They'd been Odin's servants for millennia. Had that been their plan all along? He had an image of his dad walking on the lake, two ravens circling above him.

The hull glowed, blackening and crumbling. Flames moved over the dragon's throat and the fanged mouth smoked. The boat drifted towards the centre of the bay.

Jack stared at it, remembering Petter's yearning words: "*I'd give anything . . . to really understand how they thought and felt. . .*"

The three of them watched as Tor's boat sank, leaving nothing but a swirl of ash and a ripple of gold, and the dawn sky turning a faint, clear blue.

EPILOGUE

BEGINNINGS

⚡

And its light shone over many lands.

BEOWULF

Jack stands at the frozen edge of the bay, looking out at the place where the dragon boat sank. Near the shore, paper lanterns glow in the twilight, and Jack goes forward over the ice to lay his.

One for his dad, one for Petter, one for Lukas; and one for Tor, because no one's counting any more.

Jack's mum nods at him and he rejoins her, holding on to Gran and Gramps, Gramps leaning on his stick.

More people go forward to lay their lanterns, faces fixed. Jack sees Emma's parents watching from the crowd; sees Skuli's dad. There are low murmurs, bewildered whispers, tears. There's still confusion about what happened.

That thing the adults had – some say it was a kind of virus; the kids had it too and it affected their thinking.

Not that anybody remembers much. You hear about these epidemics happening. Freak seismic stuff too. Magma shifts. And everyone knows how crazy the weather's getting.

The deaths were all put down to natural causes.

The truth? Who'd believe that?

Dear Vinnie,

Sorry it's been a few months since I emailed.

Things are slowly improving here. Gran's got the *kafé* going again, so at least there are cakes! Some of the wrecked houses are getting finished and Gramps says they'll build them even better this time round.

But it's been tough. Even when the emergency people finally got to us, they were stretched thin. Afterwards was the worst part in some ways. Digging through the rubble . . . you know.

At least Mum got pulled out from whatever spell she was under. A doctor's got work to do, she says.

I'll not be coming back for a good while yet. There's too much to help with here. But then England doesn't look much better off from what I've seen on the news.

And that stuff I told you?

Emma says one day she'll write it all in a book, use a false name. She's already thought of a title and everything! *Arrowhead*. One word's punchier, she says, and I guess that one pretty much sums everything up. Skuli told her that he reckons it'll be quicker to carve another standing stone than write a book! But Tor waited that long – what's another thousand years?!

Take care, mate.

Jack

Jack looks at the ice reflecting the twilight. He sits with Skuli and Emma on the snowy shore, each of them tying on a pair of skates. Sno runs in circles round them, snapping at the frost his paws throw up.

The frozen water glints with tiny rainbows. It looks like pearl; a sheet of silver with strings of diamonds running through.

Jack tightens his lace and stands up. "Let's go home."

He feels Emma take his hand.

The three of them step out together. Small, cautious steps at first, getting bigger, quicker, now they know the ice will hold them.

To the hall he went,
Stood by the steps, the steep roof saw,
Garnished with gold.

Beowulf

ACKNOWLEDGEMENTS

Many people supported and encouraged me during the writing of *Arrowhead*. Family, friends, thanks so much.

To writers Sarah Mussi and Caroline Johnson.

My editor, Gen Herr, and the entirely marvellous Scholastic team. Emily Lamm the Wonderful; Jessica White the All-Seeing; David Sanger for the Earl Grey tea. Artist Jamie Gregory, for another book cover beyond all expectations.

My ice-bright agent, Caroline Walsh. The Book Witch for advice on waffles.

Writer Susie Day, for website wisdom and lemon drizzle cake.

The Nordic Bakery on Golden Square, for a taste of Scandinavia in the middle of London.

Alice Swan; SCBWI friends; writer Jane Howard for mountain rescue advice.

Writer Matt Dickinson.

Tony H. of Formby Books, best local bookshop in the Viking north.

RDL. Elvie, the Siberian husky.

Honorary Norse: Silver Wolf.

My four young warriors: Isabella, Virginia, Caterina and Marco.

Professor Michael Swanton, Dr. David Breeden; Kevin Crossley-Holland for chats about Vikings at the British Museum. Curator Gareth Williams for generous scholarly advice, whilst giving scope for creative interpretation!

Anna "Chuckie-Egg" Amari; Ann Whitlock, artist and dear friend.

To Mickey S., who teaches from the heart, and who heard this one first.

And to Anna and Elena.
For showing me where the gold's buried.

AUTHOR'S NOTE

Two places inspired me to write *Arrowhead*.

The first was the evocative monastery ruins at Lindisfarne. A slaughter there in 793AD sparked the *Viking Age*, and a reputation that has held for centuries. But there's a lot more to Norse culture than bloodthirsty raids. (And Vikings never had horns on their helmets either!)

> *"This world which we think of as essentially of violence and brutality is also a world of extraordinary sophistication and cultural achievement."*
>
> N. MacGregor, Director of British Museum

Vikings were highly skilled ship-builders and seafarers, probably the first ever Europeans to make it across the Atlantic to North America. Vikings were explorers, traders and settlers, influencing our very language. They were farmers, capable of self-sufficient resilience; and craftspeople, capable of fashioning exquisite objects. Vikings were storytellers, spinning tales that still fire our imaginations a thousand years on. Stories of warrior gods at battle with ice giants; of life and death and the end of the world.

The second place that inspired *Arrowhead* was in beautiful Norway, standing by the blue ice of a melting glacier. I got thinking – what else might climate change unleash besides weird weather and rising seas? What if the Norse gods of old have been waiting, watching us, all along?

Ruth Eastham, Northumberland, 2014

USEFUL LINKS

Official website for Norwegian Tourist Board, with inspiring photos and interactive maps (with *Arrowhead*'s apologies for liberties taken with setting!):
www.visitnorway.com

Yorvik Viking Centre: Experience a reconstructed Viking settlement on the very site where excavations revealed the York of a thousand years ago:
www.jorvik-viking-centre.co.uk

How do we know about the Vikings? Article by Gareth Williams, a curator at the British Museum:
www.bbc.co.uk/history/ancient/vikings/evidence_01.shtml

National Museums Scotland: Exhibits of the Viking influence on Scotland: **www.nms.ac.uk**

National Museum of Ireland: Exhibition of Vikings in Ireland:
www.museum.ie

World Heritage site L'Anse aux Meadows; currently the only confirmed site of a Viking settlement in North America:
www.wikipedia.org/wiki/L'Anse_aux_Meadows

Wikipedia entry on the Arctic Circle and the midnight sun:
www.wikipedia.org/wiki/Arctic_Circle

National Geographic article linking extreme weather in the USA to climate change:
http://ngm.nationalgeographic.com/2012/09/extreme-weather/miller-text

QUOTES USED IN ARROWHEAD

The Elder Eddas of Saemund Sigfusson, translated by Benjamin Thorpe, 1906 (chapter 7, 11 & 18)

The Poetic Edda, translated by Henry Adam Bellows, 1936 (part 3, chapters 20 & 21)